BOOKS BY BELVA PLAIN

BELVA PLAIN

Homecoming

A DELL BOOK

Published by
Dell Publishing
a division of
Bantam Doubleday Dell Publishing Group, Inc.
1540 Broadway
New York, New York 10036

ISBN 0-440-29556-4

Reprinted by arrangement with Delacorte Press

Printed in the United States of America

May 1998

10 9 8 7 6 5 4 3 2 1

OPM

Homecoming

Chapter 1

The desktop was always covered with mail, incoming and outgoing. Appeals from charities, politicians, whether federal, state, or town, bills and letters from scattered friends, all came flowing. Sometimes it seemed to Annette that the whole world made connection with her here and asked for response.

She picked up the pen to finish the last of the notes. Her precise backhand script lay between wide margins, the paper was as smooth as pressed linen, and the dark blue monogram was decorative without possessing too many curlicues. The whole, even to the back of the envelope, on which her name was engraved—Mrs. Lewis Martinson Byrne, with her address beneath —was pleasing. E-mail might be the way these days, but there was still nothing as satisfying to send or to receive as a well-written letter; also these days, "Ms." might be the title of choice for many, but Annette still preferred to be "Mrs.," and that was that.

Having sealed the envelope, she placed it on top of the tidy pile of blue-and-whites, sighed, "There—that's finished," and stood up to stretch. At eighty-five, even though your doctor said that you were physically ten years younger, you could expect to feel stiff after sitting so long. Actually, you could expect almost anything, she thought, knowing how to laugh at herself.

Old people were amusing to the young. Once when she was less than ten years old, her mother had taken her to call on a woman who lived down the country road. It seemed, as most things did now, like yesterday.

"She's very old, at least ninety, Annette. She was a married woman with children when Lincoln was president."

That had meant nothing to Annette.

"My nephew took me out in his machine," the old woman had said. "We went all the way without a horse." Marveling, she had repeated, "Without a horse."

That had seemed ridiculous to Annette.

"So now it's my turn," she said aloud. "And yet, inside, I don't feel any different from the way I felt when I was twenty." She laughed again. "I only look different."

There she was between the windows, framed in gilt, eternally blond and thirty years old, in a red velvet dress. Lewis had wanted to display her prominently in the living room, rather than here in the more private library. But she had objected: portraits were intimate things, not to be shown off before the world.

Facing her and framed in matching gilt on the opposite wall was Lewis himself, wearing the same expression he had worn in life, alert, friendly, and faintly curious. Often, when she was alone here, she spoke to him.

"Lewis, you would have been amused at what I saw today" (or saddened, or angry). "Lewis, what do you think about it? Do you agree?"

He had been dead ten years, yet his presence

was still in the house. It was the reason, or the chief one, anyway, why she had never moved.

It had been a lively house, filled with the sounds of children, friends, and music, and it was lively still. Scouts had meetings in the converted barn, and nature-study classes were invited. Once the place had been a farm, and after that a country estate, one of the less lavish ones in a spacious landscape some two or three hours' drive from New York. They had bought it as soon as their growing prosperity had allowed. The grounds, hill, pond, and meadow were treasures and had already been promised after Annette's death to the town, to be kept as a green park forever. That had been Lewis's idea; caring so much about plants and trees, he had built the greenhouse onto the kitchen wing; all their Christmas trees had been live, and now, when you looked beyond the meadow, you saw in a thriving grove fifty years' worth of Scotch pines and spruce.

Of course, it was all too big, but Annette loved it. Especially she loved this room. It was—what was the word for it? Cozy, perhaps? No, that was a poor word to describe it. *Cozy* meant too much stuff: too many afghans, plants, and pillows. This room's walls were covered with books: novels, biography, poetry, and history. The colors were many quiet shades of blue. Today, in winter, one dark red amaryllis flourished in an earthenware pot on the desk.

In the corner there was a large dog-bed for the two King Charles spaniels. They had always kept spaniels. Roscoe, a gangly, homely mongrel with sorrowful eyes, had a mat of his own. He was completely dependent on Annette, who had found him deserted and hungry on a Caribbean beach. And she wondered whether, after having lived all these years in comfort, he had any memory of his past misery. She wondered about animals. She wondered, in fact, about everything. . . . But she had better get moving with this pile of letters if they were to be picked up today.

The morning was mild, one of those calm, cold winter mornings without wind, when the pond lay still and lustrous as stainless steel. Soon, if this cold were to last, it would freeze over. Wearing a heavy jacket and followed by the dogs, she went down the drive to the mailbox at the end.

Chapter 2

"*I* didn't say I wouldn't go, Dad. I only said I didn't feel like going."

"Cynthia, I understand. Our hearts ache for you. You can't know how much."

Across the miles she heard his sigh and saw him seated in his wing chair, high above the Potomac, with the telephone in his hand and a view of the Jefferson Memorial before him. She knew that her parents suffered as people suffer for a bomb victim or an amputee, yet still with no true knowledge of his pain.

Gran's note lay on her lap, written, of course, on the familiar paper that had accompanied every

7

greeting and every birthday present going back to the year when Cynthia had learned to read.

Come Saturday whenever it's convenient for you, spend the day with me, have dinner and stay overnight. Stay as long as you like, if you've nothing you'd rather do.

Gran was wonderful, with her sweetness, humor, and old-fashioned foibles. But Cynthia was not in the mood for them. To pack an overnight bag, to sleep in a different bed, even these simple efforts were too much right now.

"Is Mother there?" she asked.

"No, she's at one of those charity teas. Your mother, the confirmed New Yorker, has made this move from the city with no trouble at all. It's taken me, the dollar-a-year man, a whole lot longer. Government is mighty different from the business world, let me tell you."

She understood that he was making conversation because he did not want to hang up the telephone, to lose that link. He wanted to have answers to questions that usually he was reluctant to ask. Now he asked.

"I hate to bring up the subject, but have you heard anything from Andrew?"

"No," she said bitterly. "Not since the last use-less apology, and that's over a month ago, when I got my unlisted number. Apparently he hasn't gotten a lawyer yet. And my lawyer says we can't wait much longer to file for divorce."

"What the hell's delaying him?" And when she did not reply, "The bastard! And I always liked him so much."

"I know. He was likable, wasn't he? More's the pity for me."

"Tell me, are you still seeing that—doctor?"

"The shrink, you mean? No, I gave it up last week. Frankly, I find that working on meals for the homeless does as much for me, or maybe more."

"You're probably right."

Dad would think so. As a perfect exemplar of the work ethic, he disapproved of self-pity, weakness, and failure. Especially did he deplore a failed marriage. The Byrne family had never had a failed marriage. But he was always far too kind to say so. She knew that too.

"You may not think it, but this visit will do you good, Cindy. We'll take our old, brisk walk around the pond with Gran's dogs, then down to

9

the village and back. Your mother and I really want you to go. Will you?"

"What's the occasion? It's not Gran's birthday."

"She misses us. Simple as that. If you have time, pick up a box of those chocolate macaroons that she loves, will you? Your mother's bought a silk shawl for her, even if it's not her birthday. We'll take the shuttle early Friday. I'm afraid you'll have to rent a car. It's a pity you let Andrew keep the Jaguar."

"He's welcome to it. Who needs a car in New York? Anyway, he bought it, it was his money."

"Well. Well, all right, dear. We'll see you next Friday."

What was the use of arguing? It was easier to accede and go.

She sat there. Her limp hands lay in her lap. The fourth finger on the left one showed a band of white skin, as did the right hand where the engagement diamond had once flashed. You would think that after four months, skin would have darkened. And she kept sitting there, looking at her hands.

"They should be photographed," Andrew always said, "or even sculpted. You have classical hands."

He had thought she was beautiful. She knew very well that she was not, certainly not in any classical sense. She was only slender, with plentiful dark hair and fine, clear skin. She was well groomed. Working as she did on the editorial board of a fashion magazine, she understood how to make the best of herself.

"You startled me," he told her on that first evening. "I didn't want to go to another boring cocktail party, but it was an obligation. And there you were, the first person I saw when I entered the room. I just stopped and stared. You were standing there in the middle of that jostling, chattering, overdressed crowd, tall and calm in your dark-blue dress. Do you remember?"

She remembered everything. Everything. As usual she had been wearing dark blue. It was her signature. Sophisticates in New York wore black, so she would wear dark blue, different, but not too different.

"You were twinkling," he always said, liking to repeat the story, "with that look you have when you are amused and too polite to let it show. It wasn't a superior look—it isn't like you to be superior—just faintly curious, as if you were wondering what the competition and all the nervous tension were about."

Curious. Grandpa Byrne had had that look.

"I love your poise," Andrew said, "the way you don't shriek out greetings with all that fake enthusiasm people have. I love the way you can sit with your hand in mine and keep silent until the very last note of the music dies."

He had the most wonderful face, a strong nose, a soft, olive complexion, and, in contrast, light eyes, green, dark lashed and pensive. Remembering was unbearable now. A metamorphosis had taken place. What had been sweet, was gall, bitter and angry. . . .

She stood up and went to the window. New York with all its splendor was merely a jumble of towers and steeples this afternoon, a forbidding stone wilderness under the gloomy rain-soaked sky. If the rain had not been torrential, she would have gone outdoors and walked in it for miles, walked to exhaustion.

* * *

"What shall I do?" she asked aloud. "I am becoming a nuisance to myself and must not become a nuisance to other people. Must not."

Turning, she looked around the room, searching there as if, among the remnants of a life destroyed, she might somehow find a signpost, an explanation, or a direction. But the fruitwood chests, Persian rugs, and paintings of the Hudson River School with their round hills and snowfields, these tasteful possessions that befit the home of a rising young banker, all these had no explanation for the wreckage. None.

She walked down the hall. It was long, thirty-one steps to the end. Or more, if you counted from the far wall of the living room. Starting at two o'clock in the morning you could easily measure off a mile before dawn, and if you were lucky, the urge to sleep might come.

Past the bedroom where now, in a sumptuous moss-green bed, she slept alone, were the two closed doors; the people who came to clean this pair of rooms were instructed to close the doors when they were finished and to keep them so. Suddenly, she needed to open them and look in. The rooms, except for color, pink in one and blue in the other, were mirror images; each had a crib, an adult-sized rocking chair, a toy chest, and a row of stuffed animals on a shelf. Now the window shades were down, so that the light was dim, restful, and mournful, as in rooms where the dead lie. It was fitting. . . .

Remember? Yes, remember it all from beginning to end.

"Twins," the doctor said with a happy grin. People always seemed to smile at the subject of twins, as if having them were somehow, in a nice way, comical, one of nature's jokes. Well, maybe they were, she had thought, going home. And thinking so, began to chuckle.

It was an energetic fall day, and she walked briskly. In the bright air she imagined a smoky scent, although goodness only knew where it could come from, for surely here on the east side of Manhattan there were no leaves being burned in anyone's backyard. But there were chrysanthemums in the florists' windows. And she bought a bunch of miniature whites. Then, at the bakery, she bought a box of chocolate chip cookies, which would be her last such indulgence until the twins should be born. At home, having arranged the flowers on the table, she laid out their wedding silver, lighted candles, poured wine, and waited for Andrew. Working late at the magazine as she often did, she was not usually able to greet him at dinner with such a formal display.

Andrew cheered. "Great! Great! And so that's why you've begun to look like a baby elephant. To think when I married you my fingers were almost able to meet around your waist."

Kissing her lips, her neck, and her hands, telling her how happy he was and how blessed they were, he almost at once began to take charge of things.

"You are to go by taxi to and from work every day. I insist. Winter will be coming on, and the streets may be slippery, even with the slightest dusting of snow."

"You're bossing me," she protested, not meaning it.

But he was serious. "Yes, and I shall keep doing it. You take too many chances. Next thing, I swear you'll want to go skiing."

"I love your frown. It's so stern." She stroked the two vertical lines between his eyes. "I love your nice, level eyebrows and the way your hair keeps falling over the left side of your forehead. Why always the left side? And I love—"

"You silly woman. You could have found a really handsome guy if you had looked a little longer."

Plans were taking shape in his head. If we're smart, we'll start looking right now for a larger apartment. Two cribs will never fit into that little room.

Two cribs, blankets, a double carriage, and another entire layette, eventually another high chair and a double stroller, all these and more became the various grandparents' excuse to go back again to the infants' department.

Cynthia had always been gratefully aware of her good fortune. Never having been surrounded by anything else, she was nevertheless able to imagine very vividly what it was like not to have it. Going away to an Ivy League school, she felt in the first place lucky for being able to pass the entrance examinations, and after that, for being able to go without the financial pressures that bore so heavily on so many other students. Coming home at vacation time, she saw keenly how comfortable and beautiful that home was.

And there were no impediments when she and Andrew came together. Their two families, being similar, blended easily; each was pleased with its child's choice. The marriage took place promptly; since they were sure, there seemed to be little need to try each other out by first living together. So, in traditional ceremony, with Cynthia wearing her mother's lace and carrying white roses, in a grand old Gothic church, to the measures of a trumpet voluntary, they were married.

Now, with equal ease, they were planning for the arrival of their twins.

One day as spring approached, the doctor had more news. "You know what, Cynthia? You have a boy and a girl in there." He was an old man with an old man's forgivable twinkle. "You've planned it well, haven't you? That's the way to do it."

She was ecstatic. "I can't believe it. Are you sure?"

"Sure as can be."

Now there would have to be two extra bedrooms, since you wouldn't keep a boy and girl together forever. Her mind's eye, as she walked home through that warming afternoon, saw how the rooms might be decorated: cowboys in one, perhaps, and ballerinas in the other? No, too banal. As to names: both to begin with the same letter, as for instance in *Janice* and *Jim*? No, that was corny. How about Margaret, or just Daisy, which was what her mother was called, or perhaps Annette after Gran? Let Andrew choose the boy's name. There were so many lovely problems to be worked out.

This time she had a bunch of crimson tulips next to the wine cooler when Andrew came home.

"We'll need a pretty big place," he said. "Don't forget the nanny's room."

Certainly, because she would be returning to work, there would have to be a nanny, though both parents were decided that weekends were to be spent entirely with their children.

The remaining months were devoted to the new apartment. High on an upper floor from which you could see the park, this new home was one of the city's most coveted luxuries, and maybe, thought Cynthia, a greater luxury than they should have undertaken. But Andrew thought otherwise.

"It's not out of line," he assured her. "Both of us are working and doing well. And even if you didn't work, we could manage. We'd just cut way down on something else. This is an investment, a permanent home for the four of us, or maybe more?"

The birth, as predicted, went smoothly. Timothy and Laura, weighing together a total of nine and a half pounds, arrived on a breezy June day, conveniently, as Cynthia said, between four-thirty and five, allowing their father and their already doting grandparents to celebrate at dinner. Obviously, they were not identical twins, but they looked it, having Andrew's eyes, Cynthia's dimpled chin, and an unusual amount of her dark, lavish hair.

On the second morning they were brought to their pretty rooms and to the care of a good-natured nanny, Maria Luz, who had reared three babies of her own in Mexico. For the first few days there was a kind of pleasant confusion in the house, as friends arrived to coo and marvel, leaving behind them a mountain of tissue paper and shiny boxes out of which came enough tiny sweaters, embroidered suits, and dresses to outfit six babies. But eventually the house grew quiet, order was established, and a routine emerged so smoothly that you might almost think Timothy and Laura had always lived there.

They were easy babies, according to Maria Luz and the books on Cynthia's night table. They did a minimal amount of crying, soon slept through the night, gained weight on schedule, and sat up when they were supposed to.

On Sunday afternoons in the park, people turned their heads as the double carriage passed. And Cynthia, healthy and vigorous with new clothes and a flat stomach, felt that she, that all of them, had been blessed.

"I never thought," Andrew said, "I'd be so foolish about my children. I always thought that people who dragged snapshots out of their wallets without being asked were idiots. And now I do it myself."

The months went by. The first birthday came with a party, presents, paper hats, and smeared icing, all joyously recorded by the video camera. Sooner than you would imagine, the carriage was stored, and a double stroller took its place. Laura and Tim were halfway through their second year.

And now into Cynthia's mind there came a faint, unspoken shred of thought: Perhaps two were not enough? Perhaps it would soon be time to think about another? Why not? She had just been given a nice raise. Life was so good. . . .

It felt marvelous to be going home on a rare half day off with the first whiff of winter in the air. Walking fast in her sneakers while swinging the bag that held, along with her purchases, her smart, high-heeled office shoes, she would get there in time to give the baths, or one bath, at least, while Maria did the other. Tim was so active now that you had to wear a rubber apron, or you'd be drenched.

When she reached the front entrance of her building, she was still smiling at the thought. Joseph, the doorman, did not smile back, which was unusual. He looked, actually, stern. Angry about something? she wondered, and, dismissing the matter, went into the lobby. At the elevator her neighbor from the apartment across the hall came quickly forward on seeing her, and she, too, had a queer expression on her face, so queer that alarm ran down Cynthia's back.

"Cindy," the woman said.

Something had happened. . . .

"Let's go up. They were looking for you, but—"

"What is it? What is it?"

"An accident. Cindy, oh, darling, you'll need to be—"

The elevator stopped, the door slid open, and a low thrum of many voices surged toward them. Crowding there were her parents, Andrew's parents and his brother, her best friend Louise, their doctor, Raymond Marx, and—

"Where's Andrew?" she screamed and ran, pushing them all aside.

He was bowed on the sofa with his face in his hands. Hearing her, he looked up, weeping.

"Andy?" she whispered.

"Cindy. Darling. An accident. There's been an accident. Oh, God."

And so she knew. She thought she was tasting blood in her mouth.

"The babies?"

Somebody took her arm and sat her down beside Andrew. Dr. Marx was murmuring while he clasped hands tightly on her shoulders.

"There was a car, a taxi. Going around the corner, it jumped the curb."

"My babies?"

The soft murmur cut like a blade into her ears. "My babies?" she screamed again.

"It struck the stroller."

"Not my babies?"

"Oh, Cindy, Cindy . . ."

Those were the last words she remembered.

When she awoke, she was in bed. Andrew, fully dressed, was lying across the foot of the bed, which was odd. When she stretched her arm out, the sleeve of her nightgown fell back, which was normal. Sunlight fell over the ceiling, and that was also normal.

Yet there was something different. Then it all flooded; great waves of anguish and disbelief broke over her. "No! It didn't happen! It's a crazy dream, isn't it? It's a lie, isn't it? Where are they? I have to see my babies."

Andrew, trying to take her into his arms, knelt beside the bed. But she was frantic; she pushed him away and ran to the door. When it opened, a nurse in white came in with a bottle and tumbler in her hand.

"Take this," she said gently. "It will quiet you."

"I don't want to be quiet. I want my babies. For God's sake, can't you hear me?" The cry was a howl. It shattered her own ears. I am going insane, she thought.

"You must take it, Mrs. Wills. And you, too, Mr. Wills. You need to sleep. You've been awake since yesterday morning."

"Cynthia," her mother said, "darling, take the medicine. Please. Please. Get back to bed. The doctor said—"

"I want to look at them. They need me."

"Darling, you can't see them."

"Why? Why?"

"Oh, Cindy—"

"Then they're dead. That's it? Dead?"

"Oh, Cindy—"

"Who did it? Why? Oh, God, let me kill him too. Oh, God."

"Please. Think of Andrew. He needs you. You need each other."

Whether they gave her another pill or a hypodermic needle, she did not know. She knew only that the sunlight faded.

When she awoke, it was night. The lamps were lit. A few people were talking in low voices. Now she was alert enough to understand what they were saying.

The taxi, going, as witnesses said, much too fast, had smashed the stroller, which had just left the curb. The twins had died instantly. Poor Maria Luz, injured, had been taken to a hospital, treated for shock, and released. She was now staying with relatives. The children would be buried in the Byrne family plot in the country.

These were the facts. This was all. So it ended. The charmed life was over.

On the third morning Cynthia was awakened by the sound of hangers rattling on the rods in her closet.

"I'm looking for something she can wear. It will be cold." That was her mother's voice.

"You'll have to ask her. I don't know," said Andrew.

"The doctor gives her too much stuff. She's half asleep all the time."

"Just till the funeral's over. No more after that, he said."

"Well, I suppose—oh, there you are! Darling, I'm searching through your things for something black."

They were both in black, her mother in a correct black suit and Andy in the same, with the tie that he had needed to buy for his uncle's funeral. What sense did it make to care what one wore? The only appropriate thing was sackcloth and ashes, anyway.

"I never wear black," she said.

"Darling, navy blue will do very well. This wool dress, with a warm coat, will be fine. Shall I help you dress?"

"No, I'll be all right, Mom. Thanks."

"Then I'll leave you. Your father's arranged for the car. There's just time for a quick bite before we start."

"I'm not hungry."

"You must take something. Andrew, make her eat. And you eat something too."

Homecoming

"They've taken care of everything. They've been wonderful," Andrew said when Daisy left.

"Have they—I mean, are Tim and Laura—do we—"

"They're up there already. Oh, God, Cindy."

For long minutes they held on to each other. It was as if one or the other, alone, would have fallen. When at last they straightened themselves he fastened the back of her dress, she brought him an extra handkerchief, and they went out together.

In the limousine silence held almost all the way, broken briefly when Cynthia's father gave directions to the driver. Andrew's right hand, joined with her left, rested on the seat between them. Once she spoke.

"Does this seem real to you?"

In answer he shook his head. For her, reality kept flickering in through a dull sense of detachment that was equally terrifying. Was she about to lose her mind?

Reality was the memory of another time in another long limousine, not grim black like this one but white, festooned by one of their friends, a practical joker, with a JUST MARRIED sign: she had

27

worn a pale green linen suit and they had, as now, been sitting on the backseat holding hands. Reality was coming home from the hospital with one wrapped-up baby in her arms and another in Andrew's.

And she blinked hard, forcing the pictures to fade. This was no time for such pictures, going now where they were going.

"We're almost there," her father said suddenly.

The car rounded a turn and passed a parking lot filled and overflowing onto the roadside. It stopped at a walk that overflowed with people. And she wanted to flee, to hide from sympathetic eyes and soft, murmured words. Yet it was very kind of all these people to be here. So she understood what was expected of her.

She was expected to take Andrew's arm, to walk in and go straight down toward the two little white caskets. And she did so.

An odd other and outer self that had been observing her for the last two days took note of the flowers that lay in wreaths and baskets and sheaves on the floor. They, like the sprays of lilies on the caskets, were white. For purity and innocence, they stood.

But Tim had not been innocent! He had been a rogue, a rascal who stole Laura's cookie right out of her hand and made her cry. Andrew was—no, had been—boastful about his boy. "Tim is one tough guy," he always says—no, used to say. One tough guy.

The other self was watching her carefully. It told her to remember everything because this was the last day she would ever touch them or touch, rather, the flowers and the smooth white lids. She leaned forward to put the tips of her fingers on the lids. The wood was smooth as satin and cold. The lily petals were cold too.

An organ was making soft, tentative sounds like whispers or footsteps in a room where a child is asleep. When it stopped a rich, manly voice began to speak. The words were poetic and half familiar, all about mercy and love. Prayers. Beautiful, gentle words. Well-meaning. At her back there were crowd sounds, the light occasional coughs and tiny rustlings of polite, well-meaning people. She wondered when it was all going to be over.

And suddenly it was. The organ resumed its quiet song, men appeared to bear the little caskets away, and somebody said, "Come, Cynthia." Two by two people moved toward the door with Andrew and Cynthia in the lead.

Daylight burst into their faces. Following it eastward, they walked on the graveled path between last summer's stalks of dead brown grass and entered the burial ground.

Many generations of Byrnes and others among the forebears of Laura and Tim lay here in this old place. It had never been a sad place, just vaguely interesting when you were a child brought to it on Memorial Day and then most interesting when you were old enough to be curious about history. So many children were buried under these gray, time-ravaged headstones with their worn inscriptions. Molly, aged three, now with the angels. Susannah, aged two. A second summer death, most likely the result of drinking unclean cow's milk after her mother weaned her. Ethan, aged eighteen months and sixteen days. Eighteen months, thought Cynthia. Like mine. I must remember to count the days. But I can't think this minute and there is no time.

For they had reached the hole in the ground, the hole with the green drapery that was meant to conceal the stony, clodded earth which, considerately, would not be shoveled in until everyone had walked away.

The crowd had dwindled to relatives and intimates: Gran with swollen, pink eyes, Andrew's people, cousin Ellen who wept behind a handkerchief, the boss and staff from the magazine and—and I can't believe it, thought Cynthia, there's poor Maria Luz with a relative who somehow found the way here. All come to say good-bye to Laura and Tim.

Oh, my Tim, my Laura, you weren't here very long but you will never be forgotten, not your smiles, your first teeth, your long eyelashes, your cries and red cheeks and fat hands—

"Amen," spoke the fine voice, and the circular gathering responded, "Amen."

Someone, Andrew's mother or her own, or someone else, said quietly, "It's over, Cynthia."

Once more she took Andrew's hand. It was wet on the back where he had used it to wipe his eyes. The little crowd parted to let them proceed to their car. Low comments floated past them as they walked. "I heard it was the taxi's fault." "I was at their wedding." "Remarkably brave."

"Saddest thing I've ever seen." A woman looked into Cynthia's face as though she wanted to say something and didn't know how to say it.

At the end of the path they got into the car and went home the way they had come.

For a long time they held on to each other. No matter how their parents loved them and mourned with them, this agony was still Cynthia's and Andrew's. They became very solitary. They took long walks in the snow through the park, where once they had so proudly wheeled their twins, where and when the future was theirs and the world a field of flowers.

In the evenings they listened to music together. The broadcast news meant nothing to them. The apartment was completely quiet now. No more did they keep their ears open for a cry or a call. Only the great, solemn music broke the silence. Friends telephoned with tactful invitations to dinner or a movie; with equal tact they accepted refusal.

Once every week they went for a counseling session. Everyone knew that was what you did when tragedy struck. Andrew was the first to stop going.

"It's only rubbing salt in the wound," he said. "Nobody needs to tell me that I have to get on with my life. Don't I know well enough that there'll be a line waiting for my good job if I lose it?"

"What good job? We don't need any job."

"We have to eat, Cindy."

"Do we? I don't know why. I'm never hungry, and I don't care where I live. I don't need anything."

"I know. But we can't kill ourselves."

"If it weren't for you, I would."

He sighed. "Don't say that, Cindy."

"Why not? It's true." She got up and began to pace the floor, from the window to the bookshelves and back again.

"I shouldn't have been working. I should have been taking care of my own children. I'll never forgive myself, never. I look at myself in the mirror, and I see guilt written on my forehead. Yes, believe it, in big red letters: *G-U-I-L-T*."

"Darling, that's foolish. It was a ghastly accident that could have happened to you, or me, or anybody."

"You know what? I'm going to quit the stupid job. That's what I'm going to do."

"I wouldn't do that so hastily. You've taken a long leave of absence, so wait till that's over and then decide. It's too soon after—after everything to make such a big change."

It was impossible to imagine going back to that office, receiving condolences and pitying looks, being chic, being "with it," and brave. She would have to find something completely different, where there were no reminders, among people she had never seen before.

Certainly she would find something else, but not yet. She was not ready yet. And anyhow, my job is ridiculous, she thought. It has no real meaning. Fashion! Silly dresses for women who don't know what real life is all about. Hemlines are longer, or are they shorter again this season? I don't know. I know that jackets have to be fitted this year, so of course you must throw last year's jackets away, mustn't you?

She saw that Andrew was filled with pity for her. But then, her heart was broken over him too.

He didn't pace the floor for relief of tension as she did. He did not because no doubt he felt he must not. He was a man; men did not give way to grief. So they had been taught, poor souls.

At night they lay close with their arms around each other. When they needed to turn, they lay back to back, feeling the comfort of simple contact, and wanting, in their despair, nothing more than to be one.

Then, after a while, Andrew began to feel the rise of desire, but she felt nothing. "I can't," she said. "Not yet." And he complied. It was incomprehensible to her that he could feel the need for pleasure. What pleasure could there be ever again? Inside of her there was a poison, corrosive as acid, a savage hatred for the man who had killed her children and was still alive to breathe the good air; a terrible rage at unjust suffering; rage at the world.

There came a time when Andrew did not willingly comply.

"How can you feel pleasure?" she cried.

"It's not just pleasure, as you put it. It is an act

of love between you and me. We are still alive, you and I."

"How soon you have forgotten!" she exclaimed.

"'Forgotten'?" he repeated. "How can you even think that about me?"

Then she apologized. "I didn't mean it as it sounds."

"It was pretty clear to me. A simple word."

"I'm sorry," she said again, and sighed. "It's just that I can't think of anything else. I see them in the stroller, their pink faces, their little hands in mittens, so precious, and in one second—"

"Don't, don't, Cindy. You have to stop this sometime," he pleaded.

He was not always so patient. "That doctor you're seeing doesn't seem to be doing you much good."

"No? He has only saved my sanity, that's all."

There was a pause before Andrew said, "Soon it will be six months."

Six months since we last made love, he meant. And that night, when he approached her, she did not turn away, but gave herself, lying like a stone, feeling nothing.

She did not fool him, and he told her so without reproach, only with sadness.

"I can't help it," she answered.

She intended her answer to be true, and although in a measure it was true, there was another measure by which it was not true, by which she actually could have helped it but did not want to. How could they, how could Andrew, think that they would ever resume the life that had been before the tragedy destroyed it? Perhaps after all, men were different. . . .

They began to drift. When he came upon her sitting one day at the window with her hands in her lap and her red eyes swollen, he upbraided her.

"Sooner or later you will have to stop crying. I don't know how to help you anymore. We can't go on like this. I can't."

His words and his tone offended her. "And you will have to stop thrashing around all night," she cried. "I don't ever get a night's sleep. Speaking of wearing on somebody's nerves, do you realize that you're constantly cracking your knuckles? Every night we sit in front of the television, and I have to hear the sound of your cracking bones."

They went to bed and lay far apart. An emotional storm was sweeping through Cynthia. For months she had been lethargic and numb; now instead there came these storms, panic and fear of confronting love or life; panic and fear of being shut out of life. She felt a terrible, inexpressible loneliness.

She knew she must get hold of herself. She knew that they had been living like hermits, and that it was terribly wrong. So one day when a friendly couple, Ken and Jane Pierce, invited them to dinner at their country club, she accepted.

"I'm so glad," Jane said. "Frankly, I didn't think you would say yes, but I thought I'd try."

The two couples rode out of the city together, which was agreeable because conversation had to be impersonal. At the club there would be many people they knew, people from whom Cynthia had long retreated, and so, for this first appearance, she had considered her dress with special care. Is this the return of pride? she asked herself ironically. Or is it the slow return of mental health? The doctor said it was.

In the mirrored hall at the club, she saw the

reflection of a dreadfully thin young woman, with tired eyes, wearing a flowered silk dress. She had bought the dress for a vacation they had never taken; they were to have gone to Florida with the babies.

"You look wonderful," someone told her, speaking with the kindness that is reserved for people who have been dreadfully ill and who do not look wonderful.

The tables were set outdoors on a broad terrace. Without interest she ate the food that was placed before her, as without interest she heard the chatter that passed over her head. Vaguely she knew that the women were discussing a hotly fought school-board election. The men, talking business as usual, were mostly grouped at the other end of her table, while Andrew was between, with Ken on one side and a rather animated young woman wearing a rather deep décolleté on the other.

It amused her a little to see how skillfully Andrew was managing to divide his attention. He always behaved so well and had such presence. And in spite of being wan and weary he was the best-looking man here tonight. She felt sad for him. He didn't deserve what had happened to them. They must, she must, somehow turn their minds away from it. . . .

In front of Cynthia the golf course swept into the creeping dark, while to the left a wooded tract sloped gradually downhill. The day's heat still lay upon the grass and rose into the air, while overriding the hum of human voices was the clear, unending chirp of crickets.

We should have gotten out of the city long before now, she thought. It would have helped to go up to Gran's place and walk in the woods together. We must do that soon. There, we might heal. We could be what we have always been.

And thinking so, her shoulders eased; she had not realized before how rigid they were. She looked out into the distant space where twilight had turned now to full night, cobalt-blue except where Japanese paper lanterns drew their small gold circles on the darkness. How good it would be to stretch out and drowse beneath the trees! It was a long time since she had felt so sweet an urge. A curious peace had touched her, a country peace.

Andrew was laughing. It was so long, too,

since she had heard him laugh. It was so long since she herself had seen anything in the world to laugh at. Had her behavior helped to drag him farther down? Yes, probably, it had.

The woman next to him must have told a joke because all the men were laughing. She was a pretty woman, but flashy, not Andrew's type, with that heavy makeup and that dress. Not that she had ever worried about other women—for they were *married*, she and Andrew, really married.

But I have been very ill, she thought. I have certainly given no care to how I look. I need to revive, to come back to life and open my arms to Andrew.

Tonight I will break down the barrier. Tonight.

A little wind rose now, swishing through the leaves, and she pulled her shawl around her shoulders. Pale yellow wool and softly fringed, it gave her a sense of femininity and grace that she had not felt for too long. The sudden warmth within her was more than a warmth of the body; it was a lifting, a release.

And wanting to give him a look or a touch that would say, *Darling, it's going to be all right again, I'm sorry it's been so long but really, really something's just happened to me and—*

She was stopped by a long wail from Andrew's neighbor.

"My God, do you know what I've done? I've lost my best bracelet! And it wasn't insured. Oh, I'm sick."

From all sides came advice and commiseration, while people searched in the grass and under the table.

"Where did you last see it? Think."

"Are you sure you wore it tonight? Sometimes we think we had something on, and didn't."

"How did you enter the clubhouse?"

"I parked the car myself in the far lot and walked up through the front door and the dining room."

"That's easy enough. Start at the car and retrace the whole way."

"I'll go with you," offered Andrew. "We'll begin right here in the dining room. It has to be somewhere."

"Oh, how sweet of you! Two pairs of eyes should surely find it."

The men returned to their conversations. The

women talked about children, those learning to walk and those applying at colleges. And Cynthia, listening, was not devastated. It hurt, but not quite as deeply as such talk had been hurting. She was mending. . . .

Twenty minutes went by. A few people were preparing to leave.

"Baby-sitters, you know."

"Have to get up at the crack of dawn tomorrow."

"Where can your husband have gone?" Ken asked.

"I'm wondering where myself," she replied.

"Well, they went in that way," somebody said doubtfully.

Cynthia went inside to look. There were only some youngsters dancing the macarena. From the front steps she had a clear view of the parking lots. That woman's red dress would be visible. . . . She went back to the table. Fear, even as she knew how unreasonable it was, began to throb through her chest. He might have fallen somewhere or been suddenly taken ill. You never knew. The world was filled with unanticipated dangers. Who could be more aware of that than she was?

More time went by. One of the men walked to the edge of the golf course, calling a long, drawn-out "Andrew . . ."

Silly of him. What would anyone be doing out there?

"It's a puzzle," Ken said.

Jane moved restlessly. She had children at home, and there was an hour's drive ahead.

"It's fine for the people who live around here, but for us poor folk who stay in the city all summer—" She broke off. "Well for Pete's sake, we've all been looking for you."

Andrew, with the owner of the lost bracelet, was walking out of the woods, she flourishing the bracelet and laughing.

"Guess what? It was on the seat of my car. I always take it off while I'm driving. The charms get in the way."

"But where on earth were you?" Cynthia heard Jane ask, and heard another woman adding under her breath, "Where do you think? It's only Phyllis's usual little disappearing act."

And Andrew, who had certainly heard, too,

was standing like a bashful boy, startled by the sudden fall of silence.

Ken said quietly, "Let's go get the car. It's late."

"I need the ladies' room first," said Cynthia.

Jane followed her. "Don't let him see any tears, don't give him the satisfaction," she counseled.

Cynthia, replying with some defiance, for a soft response would surely have brought tears, said quietly, "You don't see any, do you?"

And she bent toward the mirror, running a comb through and through her hair, which did not need combing. A terrible shame flushed her face; she had been publicly humiliated.

"That Phyllis person is really a bitch. She can't keep her hands off a good-looking man. I don't know why anyone would want to invite her here; she's not a member."

"Oh, please—"

"All right, I'll say no more. Only, listen, Cynthia, you two have been through hell. Don't let this throw you back down. It's rotten, but it's not the worst. You just have to close your eyes sometimes."

It was unbearable. "We'd better go. They're waiting."

"If you're ready. Otherwise let them wait."

"I'm ready."

"Don't worry, you look fine."

"Do you know what? I don't care how I look."

"Men." Jane sighed as they walked to the car. "Men. They're all the same."

Andrew and Ken, together in the front seat, talked their way back to the city, while the two women were silent, Jane out of consideration and Cynthia in turmoil. She was a pitied woman whose value had been cheapened in front of strangers. The armor of marital dignity had been stripped away from her.

All these feelings came rushing into words the moment the apartment door was closed. On shaking legs she stood leaning against the wall.

"You were gone for three quarters of an hour from the time you were missed, and God knows how long before that. With that—that cheap thing that even Jane said can't keep her hands off a man—and you, you made a fool out of yourself." She was maddened. She thumped her chest. "You did this to me? To me?"

46

"I didn't mean to make a fool out of you or myself. It's—you're exaggerating. It was harmless," Andrew said, stumbling over the word. "I meant, I didn't mean any harm. Foolish, I meant."

She stared at him. Never before had he, a man of confident pride, appeared so flustered, so inept.

"Foolish," he repeated, looking not at Cynthia's face, but at her shoes.

"What were you thinking of? What were you doing there?"

"We—it was—a walk. We took a little walk."

"I'm sure. It wasn't a little walk, it was a long one, unless—unless you spent a good part of it lying down."

"I admit I used poor judgment, but you're making too much of this, Cynthia. You're carrying it too far."

"Am I? I don't think so."

Everything about his posture spoke to her and drew a picture in her head. She threw her words at him. "You had sex with her."

"That's ridiculous. You have no grounds for thinking so."

"I simply feel it. There are times when you feel

things. Anyway, what else would you have been doing, discussing philosophy with her?"

"We were just talking. Talking, about nothing in particular."

"Out in the dark bushes for almost an hour talking about nothing in particular. Do you think I'm an idiot? What's all this about, Andrew? I want to know. And don't lie. I want the truth. I can take it."

There was a silence. There were voices in the corridor as people came out of the elevator. There was silence again.

And then suddenly, Andrew raised his head. He looked straight back at Cynthia. "You said you wanted the truth. Well, what you feel—well, you're right."

All her nerves jumped. One, at the corner of her temple, shot a single, dreadful pain, and she had to sit down.

"It's probably best that I admit it, that I tell you the worst. Then you'll believe me when I say that I've never done it before."

She began to sob. "I think I'm losing my mind."

He spoke humbly. "I never have done it,

Cynthia, I promise. I must have been crazy to-night."

"Why? Why? Were you drunk? You're never drunk."

"I had a few glasses of wine, but I won't blame it on that. It simply happened. I'm so sorry, Cindy. I wish to God it hadn't."

" 'Just did.' You bastard. What would you say if I had done it?"

"I would be furious. Frantic."

"No doubt. The mother of your children. Your dead children."

"It was crazy. I don't know how else to say it, it was crazy. Because I love you, Cindy, and I always will."

She saw that his eyes were filled with tears. He moved to the chair as if to touch her hand or caress her head, asking pardon. She picked up her white evening purse and hurled it at him. It fell on the floor, breaking the fancy little frame. She was inflamed, burned alive with outrage, the image of him lying on the grass—with whom? A glittering dress and a raucous laugh.

"I hate you," she screamed. "After what we've

been through, you can do this—after what we've been to each other—or so I thought."

"Cindy, please. Nothing's changed. I've done an awful thing. But can't you forgive an awful thing, an aberration, a crazy moment?"

You never know about men. They all swear they don't do it, even the best of them.

"I admit it was inexcusable. But you have been so cold to me—"

"Cold! When my heart's been crushed! What sense are you making? Don't you hear yourself? No, you don't. You don't have the faintest idea of anything that—"

"And *my* heart? It's you who haven't the faintest idea of what it means to come together and comfort each other. I tried so, I tried all these months. I needed a little human warmth. That's all I needed." He stopped, and wiped his eyes. "I'll keep trying if you will, Cindy. Please. I'm so damned sorry about everything."

An actor, he was. Walks back to the table nice as you please after he's dusted the grass from his trousers.

"I can't look at you," she said. "You sicken

me. Go inside and get a pillow for yourself. You'll sleep here on the sofa."

"If it'll make you feel better tonight," he began.

"Tonight, you say? Don't bother counting the time until I let you back in any bed with me."

Never. Oh, God, never. Period. I'm looking at someone I don't recognize. I wish I were dead. God, let me die.

He had wrecked everything. Just when they were starting to see light, he had turned the light off. How would she ever trust a human being again? The world that had once been decent and rational made no sense. Hatred solidified into a hard mass around her heart. She floundered among moods, among sobbing grief, fury, and despair.

"But I've apologized over and over," he kept saying all through those first awful days. "I tried to explain something that's probably unexplainable. I beg you, Cynthia. I beg you now."

"A wife sitting at the other end of the table, and a man calmly walks off into the bushes. No. Beg all you want. I'm deaf to it. I don't want to hear you or see you. In fact," she said one morning after another bitter session, "the sooner you leave here, the better. Let me alone. Leave now."

"You can't mean that, Cynthia."

"But I do. I'll give you a day. I'll give you till tomorrow. You can spend today packing your things. Then, as soon as the apartment can be disposed of, I will leave it too."

"My God," Andrew said, "you do mean it." And his temper rose too. "Then sit here and stew. Cry your eyes out instead of pulling yourself together. I've lost patience. I can't do any more."

So it ended. Now she was trying to make a new life for herself at work in a settlement house for homeless mothers and children. It was a joyless life, but a useful one at least. Often she thought when she saw a young woman holding her baby that she would be willing to change with her. Poverty was cruel and dreadful, but with compassionate help it could be overcome; it was not final.

Again she went to the window as if out there might lie some answer to her questions. The sky was a dirty pink, the nighttime sky that hides the stars above great cities. It was time to leave this costly view and things that filled these rooms, the shining, pretty gadgets that once had been so joyfully assembled for a lifetime home. Gran's letter lay open on the desk. *Come and spend the day. Spend the night. Stay as long as you want to. I love you.*

Once more she read the loving words and imagined Gran at her desk writing them.

How could anyone refuse?

Chapter 3

In Washington, Lewis Byrne put down the receiver and sat quite still, thinking about his daughter.

He had always, in the privacy of his thoughts, called her his gift of joy. Tall and calm as Cynthia was, he could see himself and his kin in her; piquant and graceful, she was also like her mother, having Daisy's quick wit and strong, athletic body. Repeated in Cynthia these qualities seemed to have been intensified; as you watched her, you could imagine a bird in flight. A wounded bird now, he thought, and was heavy with that thought, when the door opened and Daisy came home.

"How was it?" he inquired.

"Nice. I surprised myself by finding how many women I already know in Washington."

"Looking at you, nobody would ever guess your worries."

She had brought a brisk air into the room, as if she had just returned from a swim or a horseback ride or tennis. There was energy in her stride and her direct blue gaze.

Ruefully, she replied, "What's the use of showing them?"

"None, I suppose. I talked to Cynthia."

"Anything new?"

"Nothing, except she's going with us to Mother's."

"Oh, that's good. I was afraid she wouldn't."

"She loves my mother."

"Well, of course. What I meant was, having to go through the town, seeing the church where they were married, and then the cemetery."

"How Andrew can have done this to her! Men have their moments, God knows, but this! It's unforgivable. After all they had been through, and just when we really thought she was beginning to recover." Lewis shook his head, sighing. "No matter how old your children are, it's never over, is it? Remember the shock we had when she broke her arm in three places? And when she was seven, and got lost at the Brownie picnic—or we thought she was lost, anyway?"

"Remember when she was fifteen and madly in love with that awful boy?"

For a few minutes they were silent, until Daisy said gently, "Get up. Let's have dinner and go to a movie, a comedy, if there is one. This sort of thing doesn't help either us or Cynthia."

"You're right. But I hate December," he said as he rose.

On a short, gloomy afternoon that call had come, rushing them to their daughter, to their dead grandchildren and the anguish.

"I know it's a bad month altogether. But come on, dear, get your coat."

For Daisy's sake he must try. They had dinner and it was good, but he was not hungry. The movie flickered before his eyes without registering. Back at home when she went to bed, he pleaded work.

"I'll come in a little while. I've got to read some material on public housing."

In the chair by the window he settled down again. The apartment must certainly be warm, he thought, since it always was, yet tonight it felt as if a chill were seeping through the walls. The Jefferson Memorial looked like a carving in ice, and the world froze. He got up, shivering, to pour a glass of wine. Perhaps it would not only warm him, but put him to sleep. These days he always felt short of sleep.

Yes, December. I shall always hate the month. As if Cynthia's catastrophe were not enough, this week is the sixth anniversary of another death: on a Saturday night the firm of Byrne and Sons died. One of the finest architectural engineering firms in the country came to an end. Smashed. Wiped out.

And at this recollection Lewis's hands shook, spilling the last few drops of wine on the unread public-housing report. A disaster like that must live forever in one's mind, he thought. He could still see the headlines in the newspapers, black letters dancing a crazy, evil dance.

"Three concrete balconies in the new Arrow

Hotel International collapse. Eighty-three killed and more than six hundred injured. Rescue workers fear many more trapped inside. Toll may go much higher."

The horror. And Gene, my brother, my partner, still blames me. No forgiveness, no understanding, just blame.

That structure—and it, too, he saw as clearly as if he were now standing in front of it—that elegant, milk-white luminescence between the palm groves and the Atlantic, was to have been, if not the firm's crowning work, then at least another triumph in its list of successes from coast to coast. Arrow Hotels International had, for the past twenty years, engaged no other firm but Byrne to design their projects. And now the glory days were over.

It had all begun with that scruffy-looking kid, Lewis thought, having an exact recollection of the morning when his secretary had announced that "some young fellow" was insisting upon seeing Mr. Byrne.

"Some kind of a nut, is he?"

"I don't think so, Mr. Byrne, although you can't always tell, can you?"

Jerry Victor was his name. The matter was very important, of great concern to the firm, and a matter of conscience.

"All right, I'll see him and get it over with."

"That's not a bad idea. He looks like the type who'll keep coming until you do see him."

He was some sort of high-level clerk in the office of Harold Sprague and Company, the contractors. Deliberately untidy, with typically uncombed hair in a ponytail, he was well spoken, very earnest, and obviously educated. You could tell almost from his first few words that he was also a crusader. Some people, and Lewis was one of them, would say at once that he was an agitator. Admittedly, Lewis was a conservative whose tolerance for what he called "cranks" was low. Nevertheless, he listened politely to what Victor had to tell.

He worked in a small space at the end of a narrow corridor between two offices. On a recent day sometime after working hours, he had gone back to his desk to get some important keys that he had mislaid. Except for a cleaning crew the offices were vacant, so it surprised him to overhear two men in conversation across the passage.

He was certain that one of them was Mr. Sprague. The voices were low, but the walls were thin. While he was searching and unfortunately not finding his keys, he could not help but overhear. He was, he said, not accustomed to eavesdropping, but he had been so shocked by the first few words, that he had then concealed himself to hear the rest.

"Then eight percent, is it?" asked one man.

"Yes, isn't that satisfactory?"

"We had talked of ten."

"That's a bit steep."

"You have to consider volume. We have two more jobs for you after this with Byrne. You'll find it worth your while."

"How about nine percent back? How does that sound?"

"Okay, okay. We'll compromise. You won't lose anything. There are more ways than one to mix concrete, right?" And someone laughed.

That, then, was the incredible story. Good God! Harold Sprague had been a friend at Yale, and before that, a friend at prep school. They had traveled in Europe together, and their families had been summertime neighbors in Maine. It was impossible to associate him with a dirty kickback scheme. This kid, this Jerry Victor, had most certainly not understood correctly and had probably not even heard correctly. Most likely he had some agenda of his own; he had perhaps been reprimanded and was seeking revenge; or he was simply a radical who lied because he wanted, on principle, to undermine a company, that being the true motive of many a whistleblower these days. So Lewis reasoned.

Or so he had reasoned then. Time and events had tempered that first certainty. Reflecting, he gazed out now upon the lights that dotted darkened Washington. No doubt, he could admit, he had been somewhat dazzled by the name of Sprague and should not have been. He winced as he recalled that day.

"This is a preposterous accusation!" he had said. "You didn't even see the men."

"I know Mr. Sprague's voice."

" 'Know his voice'! No, young man, that's pretty flimsy evidence. I suggest you forget about it, do your job, and take care of yourself."

After admonishing and then dismissing the fellow with proper dignity, he had mentioned, as if it were a joke, the absurd affair to Gene.

"All the same, it should be looked into," Gene said.

"What? You can't be serious. Do you actually want me to insult Harold Sprague with rot like that?"

"When you come down to it, what do we know about him or his suppliers? This is the first contracting job we've ever given him."

"We know his reputation up and down the West Coast."

"We shouldn't have changed. We've had the same reliable contractors for the last twenty years."

"I wanted to give him a chance, now that he's expanding in the East. His price was competitive, wasn't it?"

"I don't agree. We definitely ought to speak about this. I'll go if you feel uncomfortable about it."

"Gene, I forbid you from doing it."

Nevertheless, Gene did it.

"I was tactful," he reported a week or two later. "I said that I thought he should know there was a rumor, not that I believed it, just that he should know it. Of course he was indignant, furious—oh, not at me, don't worry—"

"I think you've made a big mistake because of a disgruntled crank."

"I don't know about that. The kid came to see me a few days ago. He's been having a tough time, and he's leaving his job."

"Good riddance. He's an arrogant troublemaker. I've asked around and found that nobody likes him. He even stirred things up in the union."

"As to that, I don't know. But I do know that I can look at a man and most of the time I can tell whether he's an honorable, truthful human being or not. I believe that boy is."

"That's a doubtful statement, Gene. Think about it."

"No more doubtful than your belief in a man because you went to Yale together."

And so, a slight distance grew between the brothers. It was nothing overt, rather a subtle coolness, as when a draft stirs the air in the corner of a room that is otherwise tight and warm. It was still remembered when, two years later, the grand hotel was finished. . . .

And what a jewel it was! Here was grandeur without ostentation, which he despised. When the lines were right, there was no need for fussy ornament.

Standing at the place where a blooming low hedge divided the lawn from the sand, he looked beyond the great arch, all the way through the depth of the structure, to the opposite arch and the alley of royal palms that stretched from the front entrance to the road. If you were standing at the front entrance, you would see only blue water and, at this moment, the black nighttime sky, in which mountainous clouds hid a few blinking stars.

It will rain soon, he had thought, probably all day tomorrow, too, and was glad for her sake that Daisy had not been able to come along this time. She had been at so many engineers' meetings, anyway. As for him, this one was rather special, since most of the members were having their first look at Byrne and Sons' achievement. He moved to go inside to the music, the champagne, and, frankly, to the congratulations.

A thunderous clap shook the air. Like lightning as it splits and fells a tree, striking unholy terror in animal or man, it crashed again. And instinctively, Lewis ran for shelter. Then in an awesome fraction of a second as he reached the door, he saw, not shelter, but chaos—and it was inside.

It struck his heart. He thought he was having a stroke. He thought he was dying.

Chaos was concrete boulders, contorted steel, and shattered glass, lying at the bottom of the five-storied atrium. The balconies had fallen. Even now, the last one on the second floor, struck by the one above, was giving way, and shrieking, flailing, tumbling human bodies were falling with it.

Now he knew he was dying, and wanted to die. There was, among all who saw this, one long, audible intake of breath; then universal screams, sobs, and curses, and after that an instant, violent, impulsive rush to aid. Lewis pulled a girl from under a girder; she had lost an arm. A man lay with blood pouring from his mouth; his eyes were open, and he was dead. Human beings, their heads barely visible beneath the rubble, cried and pleaded in terror, while groups in twos and threes strained to move the debris that covered them. Lewis thought of his brother, but there was no time or way to look for him. There was scarcely any space in which to walk through the mass of ruins.

Water came gushing from broken pipes onto the slippery floor. An enormous chunk of concrete too heavy for human arms to shove lay over a pair of legs, and yet he tried; the man was screaming in his agony and begging; then suddenly his cries ceased, and Lewis walked away to steady an old woman who, though bloody, was able to stand. A child's face was torn; he had fallen onto the sharp end of something, most likely onto a piece of the delicate iron filigree that had adorned the balconies. A gush of vomit came from out of Lewis's mouth.

On one side of the lobby little tables were still set with cutlery, flowers, and pink cloths. On the other, in the cocktail lounge, the piano stood unscathed. Beyond it you could glimpse the Blue Room, where on sofas and carpet those victims who could be extricated from the destruction were already being laid.

Chambermaids, chefs in white, and men in maroon uniforms came running in from all over the hotel. Someone said, "Come here, grab her legs," and Lewis obeyed as they picked up a heavy woman who had fainted. People ran in from the street. It must be raining, he thought, for their clothes were streaming. Dazed, he moved from aid to aid, from place to place, through the turmoil of dust and splintered glass. In one vague moment he thought he was seeing the carnage of a battlefield, read of in countless books and watched through countless movies. Only here in this place there had been music a few minutes ago, and women in evening gowns. . . .

The wail of an ambulance broke into his daze. Police, firemen, and paramedics began to take charge. More help came. In the mirrored ballroom a temporary morgue was set up for the many dead. There was a frenzy of newsmen carrying cameras.

How many hours all this went on, Lewis was never able to recall. It seemed as if days must have passed until, pushed to the limit of shock and exhaustion, he went up to the suite that had been reserved for himself and Gene.

The lobby had been cleared of the dead and

injured. They had done all that they were able to do that day. What remained was the work of the hospitals. What he did recall perfectly, though, was the terrible quarrel with Gene.

Gene had opened a bottle of brandy. "Because God knows we need it. That scene downstairs in the lobby—hell couldn't possibly be worse."

Rain spattered on the balcony. A high wind had risen, clattering in the royal palms. It had blown the outer doors open.

"Some idiot didn't latch the doors," Lewis said. He got up and locked them. "I feel angry at the world, Gene. Things like this shouldn't happen. Music one minute and amputated legs the next. Listen to that wind. All we need is a hurricane."

Gene filled his glass and sat staring at the wall. Lewis still stood at the window, trembling, staring at nothing. After a while, hearing Gene's mumble, he turned around.

"What are you saying?"

"Just mumbling. Trying to figure the count. How many do you think? Dead and injured altogether."

"I don't know. Too many, that's all I know. God almighty!" he cried. "How and why? Why?"

"I'll tell you. Because we should have taken action at the start when young Victor came with his story about Sprague. I suppose you see now that I was right two years ago. I hate having to say it, but it's the truth."

"You're jumping at conclusions. We don't even know yet what went wrong, and you've already fixed the blame for it."

"We know very well what went wrong. The concrete was no good. All you have to do is feel it. Cheap stuff. Not enough aggregate. I searched as best I could in all the mess tonight, and I'll swear there weren't nearly enough iron bars for reinforcement either. We trusted. Or you're the one who trusted. Not I! And now we'll be blamed for the disaster. The fact is, we deserve the blame."

"Well, if the supplier gypped Sprague and you're sure about the concrete, I don't see—"

"I'm sure. Go downstairs now and see for yourself. I never wanted Sprague, anyway," Gene muttered. "You know I didn't. And now we're

through, finished, washed up. Do you understand?"

"You're jumping at conclusions, as I've already
said, and you're drunk. That's brandy you're
drinking, not water."

"I need to be drunk. Do you realize how many
people died tonight? And how many may live
who will never walk again on account of your
stupidity?"

"God damn it, how dare you!"

"I dare. Your fancy friend, heaven help us.
Let's not offend him. Oh, no, never. No social
conscience, that's your trouble."

"You're out of your head. I'm not going to let
you get away with this when you sober up,
brother or no brother."

Toward dawn the telephone rang, bringing
down upon both their heads the raving rage of
the hotel's owners, Arrow Hotels International.

"You were hired because you're supposed to be
the cream of your profession. What in hell have
you done or not done with this job? You'll hear
from our lawyers at ten o'clock your time, and
we'll be at your door ourselves as soon as the
Concorde lands tomorrow."

So then we entered the prickly thickets of the law, thought Lewis now, a dark wilderness where we strayed for months and years, looking for some light beyond.

It's all a matter of passing the buck, distributing the guilt. The supplier cheating the contractor (oh, yes, I admit, Gene was right, and the concrete was inferior). The contractor is an innocent victim, or else he is criminally negligent. The architect engineers at the top of this pyramid have the same choice, as does the owning company. Victimized or responsible? Which is it? So they all sue each other. And the families of the dead and injured sue everyone in sight.

Then into the fracas steps Mr. Jerry Victor, a few years older now, with a respectable suit and haircut this time, plus an interesting story for an investigative reporter. And where does the reporter go after interviewing Victor? Of course he goes to Lewis Byrne. And Lewis Byrne is called upon to explain himself in the courtroom, to give as best he can his foolish reason for not pursuing an inquiry. And Eugene Byrne must explain his part in the affair, how he did ask his brother to speak with Sprague, and how his brother refused.

Thank heaven the business had finally come to an end.

Not, he thought now, that it ever really will. Shall I ever stop seeing the terrible face of that girl with the bloody, mangled shoulder and missing arm? Was she dying, dead, or in shock when I picked her up? I don't know enough about the human body to tell. And I still hear that old man going mad, screaming a woman's name: "Julia! Julia!"

"What on earth are you mumbling about?" asked Daisy. "I was just falling asleep when I heard you. Come to bed, it's almost twelve."

"I was thinking of things. Of my rotten brother, for one."

"Honey, you've got to stop. He's not worth your thoughts."

"All right, I made a bad mistake. But he has no understanding, no mercy. Testifies against me. Accuses me of having no social conscience. Can you imagine? Me, a dollar-a-year man? While he's still raking in consulting fees?"

"Lewis, please. You get yourself so worked up."

She was pressed warmly against his back, with

her arms around him, her lips moving on his neck. After all these years she could still give him everything he wanted. Yet tonight he was too filled with his distress to respond.

Feeling this, she withdrew, saying gently, "The last few years have been too tough. We're due now for some good years. I'm sure we are."

"Social conscience," he repeated as though she had not spoken. "That snob. He and his wife, Susan, the *Mayflower* descendant. Neither one of them ever got over that, did they? And look at the way he treated Ellen when she fell in love with Mark. Believe me, I'd choose Mark any day over our son-in-law, with all his fine family background. Even if Mark is Jewish. The things Ellen's told Cynthia about what they had to go through because of Gene! Good lord, Arthur Roth's Jewish and he's been my accountant for thirty years, and my father's before me, and he's the salt of the earth."

"Come, come, for heaven's sake, you're out of breath. This isn't doing you any good, or me either."

"I didn't tell you I saw Gene the last time we were in New York to visit Cynthia. I guess I didn't want to upset you. I saw him approaching me at the end of the block. It's a good thing I'm farsighted. It gave me time enough to cross the street and look into a shop window. I tell you, Daisy, the sight of him makes me boil."

"Then it's good that you don't have to see him. Let's try to do something about our Cynthia instead. We're going to have a good visit at your mother's. I always feel as if I've stepped back into an easier, slower age when we're there at your old home. The mahogany is cared for, there are flowers on the table, the dogs are brushed, old George still does the gardening, Jenny's still in the kitchen, and your mother's always cheerful."

At this Lewis did finally have to smile. "Yes, there's something about her that draws people. Jenny told me last time that she and George plan to stay as long as Mother lives." Then, frowning again, he exclaimed, "Poor Mother. She shouldn't have these family troubles at her age. I wonder—do you think maybe she's asked us to come because there's something wrong with her? She's the last person to complain, but if there is anything wrong with her health, I'm glad it's me that she wants to see. God knows she wouldn't get the same help from Gene."

"Darling, I'm sure there's nothing the matter. She simply wants to give Cynthia a little change. It's going to be lovely for the three of us. Come on to bed."

Chapter 4

The first thing Gene Byrne noticed when he came home from his office was the topmost envelope in the pile of mail on his desk. Anna, his day worker, had known he would be interested first in his mother's letter.

Sitting down at once to read it, he had to smile. An invitation to spend the day and stay for dinner! It could just as well have been given over the telephone. But then, that would not have been like his mother to do.

"I would appreciate your not mentioning this to Ellen. I don't want to hurt her feelings. Do I have to tell you how I adore your Ellen and her babies? I do plan to have them come soon, but this time I'd like to have just you."

The indefatigable Annette Byrne is finally showing her age, he thought. Young children, especially his darling granddaughter Lucy, can wear even a young person's nerves out after a full day of their constant dartings, spillings, and questions. He understood that, and yet he was disappointed. Although his days were filled with welcome work, and although, living as he did in New York, he could have filled his evenings, and often did so, with drama and music, he had his lonely hours too. His life had changed when his daughter married, his son moved to London, and his wife died. He had to expect some lonely hours and had no right to complain. He never did complain. Still, he was disappointed.

Anna had put his dinner in the warming oven for him and, knowing his tastes, had set a place at the little table overlooking the East River. It was pleasant while eating to watch boats going by, pleasant to be snug here high above the windy streets, pleasant to take his drink out of a crystal goblet. The embroidered place mat was initialed *SJB*, for Susan Jane Byrne, and was still in use even though it had been bought for her trousseau some thirty-two years ago.

Susan had left him much too soon. Cancer wasn't choosy about the ages of its victims. It would be ten years next week since he had taken up what they used to call "bachelor quarters," directly after her death and Ellen's marriage, which had come a few months later. He often thought that if she had to die, she had at least been spared some unlooked-for troubles: the woeful marriage and the disaster of the grand hotel.

He himself tried not to think about those things. Fortunately, he was busy, unlike that brother of his, who had, he supposed from the little he heard, relapsed into idleness. One had to accept accomplished facts. Ellen's marriage, for instance, could have been much worse than it had seemed at the beginning. The children, of course, were wonderful. As to the other blot on his reasonably fortunate life, having had good parents and a beloved wife, he knew that it could never be wiped out. He must simply not look back at it.

That would be difficult this anniversary week, however. Yesterday, coming home in a torrent of rain, he had had a total recall of the tropical storm that night, the dripping ponchos on the cops, the shine of wet pavement where the ambulances were being loaded, the frenzied bustle, calling, shouting, and the clatter of helicopters overhead.

No more room in the morgue. They're laying them on the floor.

It should never have happened. It was, when you came down to it, simply a question of honor and truth. If only Lewis had listened to him when Jerry Victor came with his story, it never would have happened. But Lewis was too impressed with the Spragues and the château in France, where the elder Hanson-Spragues entertained ambassadors and financiers each summer, to open his mouth and investigate.

No one will ever convince me, Gene thought now and probably for the thousandth time, that Victor wasn't telling the truth. It's not as if he was looking for trouble. He could have filed a complaint for violation of the whistleblower law. He'd been promised a raise, and then all of a sudden it was denied. He'd been given some work that he'd never been taught to do and that he was bound to bungle. They wanted him to bungle it. He knew he was being prepared for a fall. Why didn't he sue? Because, as he said, he had a life to make. I admired him.

The funny thing is, if he had looked the way he looked in the courtroom a few years later, Lewis might have paid more attention to him.

He gets a lot of this snobbery from Daisy too. And who on earth does Daisy think she is? Her family never amounted to a hill of beans. Nobody ever heard of them. When I think of Susan, so unassuming even though she was the closest we come in this country to an aristocrat, going back to the *Mayflower*—

Yes, but it's Daisy's daughter who made the good marriage, not ours. Life's little quirks. You never know what's around the corner. That was a terrible, unspeakable thing that happened to those twins. I was relieved to be in London when it happened; the funeral must have been awful. Ellen said it was. I can imagine. Or rather, I can't. Suppose it had been Lucy and Freddie, I think I'd go out of my mind.

They're so beautiful and so smart and so sweet. They look like Ellen. Not that Mark isn't a nice-looking young man. He dresses neatly, very well, in fact. Of course, you have to make a proper appearance when you work in a fine midtown art gallery. I wonder how much he makes. It can't be much, I think, or why would they live in a re-modeled loft way downtown instead of up here in this neighborhood, near the park, where Cynthia lives? It's so depressing downtown among those lofts and factories, so gray and grimy, with all the trucks and cluttered sidewalks. You feel as if the air is poisonous, and it probably is, from the ex-hausts, and no trees to absorb anything. Where in heaven's name are the children going to play? And whom are they going to meet?

But Ellen's apparently quite content, so maybe the choice is her idea. I don't know. She always was an independent. Like most artists. Maybe she'll actually make a name for herself someday after the children are both in school. I saw some-thing rather good on the easel that she keeps on the north side of that big room. Good Lord, they cook and eat, she works, the children play, and they all do everything but sleep in that one room. Still, they're obviously happy together.

That elopement almost gave me a heart attack.

Why, with all the contacts and opportunities she had, did she have to pick anybody named Mark Sachs? Not that I have anything against Jews. Well, maybe I do, a little. They're peculiar people. I never know what they're thinking. I don't feel at ease with them. It's just—it's just— Actually, though, it's not Mark whom I mind so much. No one could say fairly that Mark is not a gentleman. But his parents, especially his father! Never mind that he's a doctor and supposedly chief of some staff somewhere or other, I can't look at him. The one time I saw him, nine years ago, was more than enough. I never want to look at that black beard again. Sat there with a sour face; didn't eat anything. Ellen promised I wouldn't have to see him, and thank heavens, she's kept her promise. I daresay the doctor isn't eager to see me either. Hah! It was mutual hatred at first sight, especially on his part. I sensed it the minute he walked into the room. The mother isn't quite as bad, except for her loud, whiny voice. Overemotional. Orthodox. Not pleased with my daughter. Not good enough for him. I can imagine how they must have ranted at home. To be mixed up with people like those. And my grandchildren related to them, tied to them for life.

I'll bet he hasn't given them a cent because he disapproves of the marriage. At least I've set up trusts for my family that they don't even know about. I'd like to give them things now, but they won't accept anything. Ellen doesn't want anything, and Mark's very independent. Well, I give him credit for that. So they'll get theirs when my time comes. Except for Susan's jewelry. Ellen already has it all, some handsome pieces, too, although goodness knows when she ever wears them. At least she has them. It wouldn't have hurt those people to make a gift to the mother of their grandchildren, even though they don't like her. Oh, well. As long as I never have to have any contact with them, and I won't. That's one thing you can be sure of.

Gene drank his coffee. Again, his glance fell on his mother's letter. And again he wondered whether there was any reason for concern.

Come early, she had written. *I'll expect you not later than ten.*

Well, that was all right. An early riser, he would have a quick breakfast and start. But why specifically at ten? Unless she was expecting a conference of some kind with a doctor or lawyer, perhaps. It hurt him to think of her with either one, for doctors and lawyers almost always meant some kind of trouble. She had enough worries already: Cynthia's troubles, and then the irreconcilable breach between her sons.

He got up and wrote a memorandum: *Stop at bookstore for Mother. New book on English castles, plus a good novel. Also, chocolate macaroons, large box.*

Chapter 5

On the other side of Central Park, Aaron Sachs and his wife, Brenda, were having their supper.

"We'll have to start early to pick up Mark and Ellen downtown before we get on the road," she said.

"Why they don't have a car, I'll never know. You'd think he could at least afford a cheap car."

"I'm sure he can. But what does anyone want with a car on Manhattan Island?"

"Right as usual, dear wife." And Aaron winked at her.

She was so reasonable that she sometimes,

when he was in a bad mood, annoyed him. Still, after all these years, she was his treasure, his "woman of valor," good natured, vigorous, and almost as pretty as she had been on their wedding day.

At present he was not exactly in a bad mood, but he was tired. He had had some tough surgery and a sorry case that was bound to go wrong. Now this letter from Annette Byrne was a complication in his busy life. Who wanted to drive out into the country in the middle of winter to visit a woman one scarcely knew? They had been in her house only once before, and that was nine years ago. He picked up the letter and, propping it against his dinner plate, stained it with tomato sauce.

"Oh, that beautiful stationery," Brenda said.

"Never mind the stationery. *It would mean a great deal to me if you would all come,* she says, *and it will be fun for Lucy and Freddie. We have a new family of swans to show them. So please do come.* Now, why should it mean a great deal to her? Why?"

"What's so puzzling? She's old and alone. She wants to have some time with her grandchildren and her granddaughter's family. Personally, I think it's very gracious of her to include us."

"We are Mark's parents, aren't we?"

"Even so."

Aaron sighed. "I won't be able to eat the food, you know. It'll probably be baked ham."

Brenda laughed. "Of course it won't be. But whatever it is, we can eat vegetables. That's what we always do, isn't it? And we can do it again."

"They don't know how to eat, anyway. The food has no taste."

"That's why everybody goes to French restaurants, the food's so bad."

"I was only kidding, my literal wife." And they both laughed.

"She's a lovely woman, very simple in her manner, as I remember her. I have to admit, though, that I'm a little intimidated. I'm not used to grandeur. Not that the house is palatial, just the reverse. It has the kind of simplicity that costs a fortune, you know? And then the grounds, the gardens—"

"Anybody would think to hear you that you live in a hovel. Five rooms on Central Park West. Not too bad."

"I didn't say it was bad, idiot."

"Then act accordingly. Don't be humble. You're an aristocrat, aren't you?"

"Some aristocrat."

"You grew up in a house in the suburbs, you went to a private school, and your grandparents were born in this country. I lived in Washington Heights with the rest of the refugees, and borrowed the money for medical school. So by my standards you're an American aristocrat."

He loved to tease her. She was so earnest, so literal minded, that he could always count on at least four or five seconds between the time she heard what he said and the time she realized that he was joking.

"Mark loves her, you know. He's mentioned her lots of times."

"Who? Ellen? He should love Ellen. He married her."

"Oh, Aaron, you know very well I meant the grandmother. She's very close to them. But the two sons haven't spoken to each other for years, Mark says. It must be a very difficult kind of balancing act for her."

"WASPs. They've no sense of family."

"That's ridiculous. You shouldn't use that word, anyway. A wasp is a mean insect."

"Well, Anglo-Saxons, then. I've nothing against them—well, maybe I have. Some. They're a cold people. And stingy. They don't do a thing for their children once the children are grown and out of the house. I wonder whether her father knows about the pearls you gave Ellen, and what we've set aside for the grandchildren. Living in one of their homes must be like living in an icebox. They don't express themselves. They walk around whispering politely, all buttoned up. No feeling."

"Nonsense, Aaron, you don't know anything about them. Those are ugly stereotypes; that's all they are."

"I know about people."

"No, you don't. You only know about people's broken bones. How can you talk like this when your own daughter-in-law is the sweetest soul on earth? And you know she is."

Brenda's fine, dark eyebrows rose, as, waiting for a response, she watched him. Yes, he did like Ellen. She was making his son happy. . . . But how much different it would be if, for example,

Mark had married the Cohens' daughter. She was a beautiful girl, and he had always hoped that something might come about. Or if not Jennifer Cohen, at least somebody from a family that could be joined to theirs. They'd celebrate the holidays together and feel at ease. What was he going to talk about up there at that fancy country estate? And he grumbled something inaudible to Brenda.

"You're tired," she said.

"I am not," he answered, never wanting to admit that he was.

"Yes, you are. I can tell by your grumble. You're tired, and this invitation has upset you besides."

"Well, it's made me think. It's brought back things that I've tried to bury. Why, Mark doesn't even go to the synagogue anymore. I asked him."

"Mark knows who he is. He discusses it freely. He's Jewish, but secular."

"Secular! Where in blazes is the good in that?"

Brenda sighed. "Where the good is, I can't answer. It doesn't seem like much good to me. But it's life, the world today, or part of it. And there's nothing you can do about it."

"I wonder what's going to happen to the children. Look at them. So beautiful."

In a double frame on the piano, they sat: Freddie, not yet two, was holding a ball, and pleased with it, smiled, showing his tiny teeth; Lucy, just six, had light, ruffly hair and a ruffly dress; her smile was piquant, already feminine.

"They both look like my mother," Brenda said. "Take after her side."

"So beautiful," Aaron repeated, his eyes going moist. "Yes, but what's to become of them, what will they be?"

"I suppose Ellen's side thinks about it too. At any rate, there's nothing we can do about that, either, Aaron."

For a few minutes neither spoke. The little table on which they had their meals had been placed at the window so that they might look down at the park. From this height the skating rink looked like a mirror speckled with moving black dots.

"It doesn't seem cold enough to be skating," observed Brenda.

"Artificial ice."

"Did I mention that Ellen's painting is going to

be shown in one of those galleries near their apartment?"

"You told me."

He knew she was making conversation. His morose humor, his dwelling on the old subject, were not fair to her. And forcing a bright tone, he said, "I think she has talent. Those landscapes she does are really pretty."

"That's just what's wrong with them. They're too pretty. They're only skillful imitations of Winslow Homer's country scenes. She even has a deer in the last one."

"Don't disparage it. I liked it."

"Darling, excuse me, you're a marvelous surgeon, but you really don't know the first thing about art."

Aaron waved his arm toward the farther wall, on which, above a grouping of stainless-steel-and-leather chairs, there hung an enormous painting of acid-green and bloody-purple tubes, snaked around each other.

"And you do? And that's art? It looks like intestines."

"Aaron! It happens to be very, very fine art."

"Bunk. You're reacting against a reaction. You

like this abstract stuff because your parents ridiculed it." And he laughed, glad to have something to laugh about.

"Well, laugh away. It's good to see you being funny."

"Incidentally, how is it that you admire Annette Byrne's things? If you like the stuff in this room, you can't like her Chippendale."

"Well, I don't like Chippendale. But her things are good of their kind, and they're put together with taste." She reflected, "Ellen has taste, too, along with her other good qualities."

Aaron nodded. "True. True. Listen, you don't have to persuade me to go. Save your energy. I'm going next week. I don't look forward to it, but I'll do it. Call up and tell her we'll be there."

"No, I'll write. When you receive a letter, you answer with a letter. That's proper. They're very proper people." And suddenly, a dark expression passed across Brenda's face. "You know what? It's only the father who puts a bad taste in my mouth."

"You just met him once."

"Yes, and that was once too often. I felt such

anger, the only time in my life I felt such anger. It stuck in my throat. I hated him."

"The feeling was mutual, you can be sure."

"Shriveled like a prune, his dry lips, and his eyes like pins pointed into my eyes. Who does he think he is, the duke of Westminster or somebody? The duke would be more gracious."

"Not if his daughter had run off and married our son, Brenda dear."

They both laughed. Then Brenda said seriously, "If I should ever run into him someplace, I'd—I'd make a scene. I don't know what would happen."

"You'd get your name in the papers, that's what would happen. Not that I wouldn't mind joining you. He looks down on our Mark! Mr. Hitler. He only needs a mustache to look like him."

"Tell me. How does a girl like Ellen come from such a father? And how does a woman like Annette have such a son?"

"God knows. Maybe it's in the genes. Don't ask me, I'm not a psychiatrist, or God either." Aaron stood up and shoved his chair toward the table. "Come on, enough of this. If you still want to go to the movies, I'll stack the dishes in the washer while you repair your face. Hurry, or we'll be late."

"Aaron, I just had a horrible thought. You don't think she'd have that man there, would she?"

"What man?"

"Ellen's father."

"Are you out of your mind? Of course she wouldn't. By the way, don't forget to pick up a little something to take along."

"I know. Mark told me what bakery to go to on the East Side. Annette likes chocolate macaroons."

Chapter 6

At four o'clock in December, the short, dark afternoon was over. Electric light filled the enormous room, glaring above the rug on which Freddie played with his blocks and Lucy, sprawled on her stomach, studied the first-grade reader. It shed a softer light on the easy chairs and bookshelves at the far end of the room, brightening the easel with the unfinished painting at the north window. And, at the opposite end, it brightened, too, the stove, the sink, and the ironing board, where Ellen was at work.

Despite the short afternoon it had been a long day. The days began around six o'clock when, from the other side of the partition that divided one space into three small sleeping rooms, there sounded Freddie's early stirrings in his crib. First came a chirping sound, part speech and part song; what thought could he be expressing and from what heard music came those few sprightly notes? Next came the rattle and pounding of the crib as he propelled it back and forth against the partition. Last came his demanding call for attention, meaning a diaper change and breakfast. There was no use, even on a holiday or Sunday, in covering one's head with the blankets, no escape from that demanding call. It was time to get up.

"Rise and shine," Ellen's father used to say when it was time for school. And now that was her own morning greeting to her own children. Funny, she reflected, how you trail all these tag ends, this miscellaneous baggage, along, even when you move from your first life into another one that's removed one hundred eighty degrees.

She still used her mother's linen place mats, even though she had to iron them herself. They were too precious to bring to the Laundromat, as were the handmade dresses that Gran bought for

Lucy. Lucy had few occasions to wear them, but they were lovely. Ellen had worn such dresses herself when she was growing up in a long-ago time of children's concerts and Upper East Side birthday parties with crepe-paper hats and loot bags to take home.

This was another world in which she lived now. It was hardly a world of poverty—not by any means—but it was surely different. Here expenses mattered very much. You had to watch them, to make some careful calculations before spending anything at all. It bothered her father, who was always questioning, always offering to buy, to pay for this or that, and always meeting with refusal. Mark's parents did the same and, in the same way, met refusal.

For Ellen and Mark had need to prove themselves. When people marry each other in stubborn defiance of a hundred earnest objections and dire warnings of failure, they must go it alone. They must show—and always she had to smile at the old, trite, true slogan—that "love conquers all." Well, of course, sometimes it did not. And she would think, then, of her poor cousin

Cynthia. But for Mark and herself, love had conquered.

And she looked over at her children. Born of love, they were blessed besides with intelligence and good looks. Their savory dinner of chicken pie and vegetables was baking in the oven. Their father would soon be coming home. What more could anybody ask for?

Her ears, as evening approached, were always alert to the sound of the rising elevator, which had once, when this building was a warehouse, carried freight and was slow. Mark's footsteps would rush through the outer hall; he seldom walked, but almost always ran to any of his destinations. She would open the door, and there he would be with his kiss, his smile, and his tie already torn off.

He was the kind of person who was most comfortable in jeans and sneakers. Anybody who knew him well would be amused to think of him or to see him at work in that uptown gallery, wearing the fine dark suit and striped tie of a banker or Wall Street lawyer. But he loved the work, and as he said, "The clothes go with the territory." As it happened, he wore them very well. He was tall and slender, with a serious expression; he was cordial and serious, with a well-modulated voice. In a word, he was elegant.

Gran said that they made a handsome couple. No one but Gran had told them that; friends do not usually make such comments among themselves; and from their respective families, given the circumstances, they could hardly expect such a compliment. Nevertheless, Ellen knew it was true. They did make a handsome couple.

She also was tall, and had once been as blond as Lucy now was. She wore her tan hair with its few clever streaks in a ballerina's upsweep, revealing her long neck and graceful profile. On her various errands around the neighborhood, marketing, walking Lucy to and from school, and taking Freddie to play in the pocket-sized park, she wore jeans as almost everyone else did. Otherwise, she wore simple clothes in vivid colors, for she loved color: aquamarine, apricot, and lapis lazuli. She wore little jewelry, inexpensive earrings that she bought in novelty shops, the plain wedding band that matched Mark's wedding band, and, on appropriate occasions, the splendid pearl necklace that his mother had given to her. It had been in essence a kind of peace offering from Brenda when Lucy was born. She liked Brenda, who had, in spite of all, a fundamental tolerance and heart.

Her own mother's jewels, which had naturally come to her, were in a safe deposit box at the bank. They were too formal and too precious to fit into Ellen's life as they had into Susan's. Lately she had come to think and speak of her mother as "Susan"; it made her seem young and filled with the happiness she must once have had. People had always described her with the word *sunny* before the long illness that filled Ellen's memory of her as "Mother" or "Mom."

If Susan had lived long enough to see us married, Ellen thought, I would have asked her some questions. And I believe I know what she would have answered. Or maybe, given the pressure that Dad would have put on her, she would not have answered. Yet I do think she knew what was happening and simply did not have the physical strength to take a stand for me. I really sensed that, didn't I? And wasn't that why we waited, Mark and I, until she died? She had enough to bear without the addition of a social scandal, absurd and minor as it was. . . .

After working hours, or on a free Saturday that first year after her graduation from college with a degree in fine arts, she used to tour the art galleries from the tail end of Manhattan to the treasure houses of the Upper East Side. Sometimes she merely glanced into a window and, seeing nothing to tempt her, walked on. At other times when tempted, she went in without any intention of buying, merely of satisfying her avid eye.

In particular she loved old landscape paintings or current works that gave the feel of a quiet world without industry—although such a fondness reflected only an impractical nostalgia—a world of greenness and space, of domestic animals, and crops and changing seasons. This nostalgia had probably to do with long summers in her childhood at Gran's house. No matter. And so it happened one spring day that she walked into a certain gallery on Fifty-seventh Street.

A very nice-looking young man came forward and addressed her. "May I show you anything?"

Ellen hated that. She had simply wanted to look, and she said so.

"Very well. I'll be happy to answer any questions you may have."

She walked around. The walls were hung with superb paintings, sparkling out of exquisite gold frames that in themselves cost more than Ellen could afford. At home they had expensive paintings, but they were not her taste. And anyway, they belonged to her parents, not to her. Standing in front of a woodland brook under falling snow, she thought: Now, I would give my eyeteeth to own that—or better still, to be able to paint it.

There were two rooms. After she had slowly and carefully passed around all their walls, she returned to the brook and was still standing there absorbed in the winter light and the stillness through which she seemed to be hearing the trickle of water over rocks, when a voice in back of her spoke.

"That really talks to you, doesn't it?"

"Yes, and I'm answering it," she said.

He laughed. It was a small, discreet laugh, professional sounding as befitted his role. There was a dignity about him, a bit formal, a quality that she took to be British. She knew very little about things British except for what she had seen on her only visit to Britain, and, naturally, what one saw on television or in the movies. Later she learned that indeed he had been wearing an English suit, bought for him by his parents on their trip to Britain. But that was another story.

"Is there anything you would care to know about it?" he asked.

"Well, yes, the price," she said, which, having been a fine arts major and having recognized all the names on all those walls, she could easily estimate.

"It is thirty-five thousand dollars. An exceptionally fine example of his work. He died last year, you know."

"Yes, I know."

"His prices are bound to go up, so this is actually a remarkably good investment."

She did not reply. The young man had lovely eyes, extraordinary eyes, brown, but yet almost gold around the pupils. Or perhaps it was the light slanting in from the street?

"Of course I understand that you would only purchase a work like this out of love for it, but still, it is always nice to know that your investment will hold up."

He wanted so much to sell it! Naturally; they worked on commissions. The place was hardly busy, either, and there were two other men standing and sitting, the latter idly turning the pages of the catalog. It must be a difficult life, very frustrating.

"I'll think about it," she told him, aware that he must, hundreds of times, have heard the same words from people who were only looking.

For an indecisive moment they stood there; she saw his glance fall to her hand, to the dazzle of Kevin's four-carat round-cut diamond engagement ring. When he spoke, there was a touch of hope in his tone. After all, a young woman who owned such a ring—might she not also do more than just think about that snow falling in the woodland brook? Bowing almost imperceptibly, he gave her his card.

Mark Sachs, she read.

"Ellen Byrne. I'll think about it," she repeated. "And thank you so much."

She walked slowly home up Fifth Avenue, where there were no shops, only the summery park on the left with its carriages, beautiful babies in fashionable strollers, and beautiful dogs being led by professional dog-walkers. On the right, all the way to the museum and beyond, rose the limestone walls of apartment houses with green awnings and doormen in maroon uniforms. In one of these she still lived with her parents, there being no sense in setting up an apartment of her own when she was so soon to be married anyway.

It occurred to her that most likely she would be spending her life in just such an apartment, spacious, quiet, and filled with valuable possessions in simple good taste. Her children would be reared as she had been, sledding in the park and sailing a marvelous boat, given for her seventh birthday, in its pond. Late in the afternoons they would do their homework in their little bedrooms above the side street; the important rooms, living room, library, and master bedroom, would face the park.

The master bedroom. The term had a masterful sound, almost patriarchal, when you thought about it. And thinking further, it seemed to fit Kevin, who was authoritarian, competent, and very kind, as well.

On first meeting him her father had observed, "That young man will go far."

He had already done so. Although not yet thirty, only four years out of law school, he had been offered a place in the firm's Paris office. At this moment he was in Paris getting some orientation, after which he would return, they would be married, and go abroad to live for two or three years; then after that, following the usual track, he would return to the New York office and a promotion.

The prospect of living in France had thrown Ellen, as in a sudden analytic mood she now saw herself, into a kind of rapture. An adolescent rapture. Ever since having been there once with her parents, she had sustained a long love affair with France. She had also sustained a love affair with Kevin.

They had been casually introduced on the campus of the university at which she was an undergraduate senior and he a graduate of its law school. He had come back that day on a visit. A group of five or six, Ellen's roommate among them, was on its way to the coffee shop, and she went along. Beside Kevin there was one other man, but he was uninteresting. It was Kevin, blue eyed and bold of feature, who held attention, not only the women's, but even the men's in the class.

He had already entered the world, that world which often, at worst, appeared like a dangerous jungle, or at best, like a game of musical chairs, where everyone scrambled, knowing that there were not enough seats to go around and that somebody was bound to be left out. Looking at Kevin, you felt almost certain that he would not be one of those left out.

Ellen had never expected to be noticed. She had indeed gone out a great deal with many differing types of men on the campus—fraternity men, athletes, and poetic loners—but they had all been her own age or close to it, so it was with a little well-hidden gasp of surprise when, under cover of some loud general conversation, she heard Kevin ask for her telephone number.

Her roommate was equally surprised. Her quick, appraising glance at Ellen seemed to be saying: Why you? What is it about you that's so special? She was, however, in possession of some interesting facts about Kevin, which she gave to Ellen. He came from an Ohio family that had something to do with steel. In New York, where he lived alone, he had an apartment near the World Trade Center.

"He will probably never call you," the roommate predicted. "He's too full of himself to bother with an undergraduate. You're too young for him."

But he was not "full of himself"; he was, as it turned out, most modestly understated, and he did call. When the telephone rang a few days later, it was to ask her when she would be back in the city. For Christmas vacation, she told him, and gave him her number there. Her father noted with unusual approval that he did not "pick her up" in the lobby downstairs, but came straight to the apartment to introduce himself to her parents.

"Which is what a man was always expected to do, you know."

Things moved with remarkable speed after that. On the first time they went to a Broadway show. On the second they danced in the Rainbow Room. On the third time they had dinner quite far downtown in one of the newest French restaurants that had gone to the top of the critics' list. The lights were hazy, the murals transported you, depending on where you looked, to the shores of Brittany, or southward to the Alpilles, and the tables were far enough apart for intimate conversations to be held in private.

It was not that their conversation was what you would necessarily call "intimate." It was explanatory. Ellen learned that he was already fluent in three languages and was trying to find time for the study of Mandarin, because China, whether we liked it or not and he did not, was sure to become the dominant force on the planet. Kevin learned that she was hoping to get a wonderful position in a major museum of art somewhere, practically anywhere, because such jobs were hard to get. At any rate, she was bound to enter the world of art; she loved it ardently, and though really she had no talent to speak of, had even tried drawing and painting on the side. They had kindred interests and some acquaintances in common.

All these things in an odd, vague way made him less a stranger, so that when they could no longer keep sitting at table drinking wine, of which Ellen was not particularly fond because it made her sleepy, followed by coffee, which woke her up—when they positively had to leave to stand outdoors in a blast of icy wind and he suggested that they warm themselves in his apartment, it seemed like a perfectly reasonable thing to do.

In those years, she often thought later after she was married, people had been amazingly casual about having sex. Quite simply, going to bed together after a few days' acquaintance was expected, even if you did not especially want to do it. Ellen really did not want to; no one had moved her deeply, as you were supposed to be moved; she wondered whether possibly no one ever would.

Kevin was gentle, yet not too gentle. He thought she was absolutely beautiful, absolutely wonderful, and told her so, over and over. Then he took her home in a taxi, saw her to the door, kissed her, and the next day sent her a magnificent bouquet of two dozen roses.

Maybe the roses were really too obvious. If I were a parent, she thought, I would put two and two together. But her mother had just had another chemotherapy treatment and was too miserable to notice anything, while her father, she guessed, was so taken with Kevin Clark's person and status that he would question nothing. Anyway, there was nothing he could do about the situation, and undoubtedly he knew it.

You grow quickly attached to a person who glorifies you, provided, naturally, that the person is otherwise attractive. When she was back at college Kevin's nightly telephone calls gave her something to anticipate all day and something to look back upon with a sense of fulfillment. As often as possible she now went home for weekends, which was something she had never done before. Once Kevin drove up for a weekend, and they spent a few hours at a motel, which was also something she had never done before.

"Ellen's a simple girl," said those who knew her best. "She has always had very few wants."

Now suddenly she wanted life to be lavish, not in any material sense, but in the amorous and sensual. Reliving evenings that her parents assumed were being spent at the theater or similar places, she bought expensive underwear and perfume. She knew she was envied, except perhaps by her radical feminist friends.

She went through finals, did very well, and was

graduated in May. She had invited Kevin because he said he wanted to come, so there he stood with her parents and Gran, among the crowd that saw her go past with the robed academic procession. Everyone knew, yet properly, no one ventured a word about what was coming next.

It came in Kevin's apartment later that week. On the twenty-second floor she was looking out at the view, the spread and sparkle across the Hudson, north to the bridge that spanned it and south toward the tip of the island, where it met the bay.

"It seems," she murmured, "that in this city, the first thing people want in an apartment, if they can afford it, is a view."

"That depends. This has been nice for me, but for the long pull I like the kind of place where you live, lower down and near the park, so our children could play there, the way you did."

She turned about. This was the greatest moment in her life, she thought. Why didn't she cry or feel something incredible? She felt merely pleased, quite pleased. But it was, after all, no surprise. She threw her arms around him, and they kissed, a very long kiss.

"I take it the answer is yes. And with that in mind I came prepared. Here it is."

"It," of course, was the brilliant ring, the family ring that had been kept for Kevin's bride. Now everything was sealed, sealed and soon to be signed. They would have to wait not quite a year until he should be established in Paris. In the meanwhile he would have to be traveling back and forth for the firm to other parts of Europe. And in the meanwhile there was great rejoicing. His parents arrived from Ohio, were invited to a celebration dinner, and to another one at Gran's place in the country. There were champagne and flowers; there were toasts. A lucky man, Kevin was. A lucky woman, Ellen was.

She was very well aware of all that on the day she walked home after the encounter in the gallery on Fifty-seventh Street.

Her mother was resting on the sofa in the library. Almost every afternoon during this past year she rested. And still, not wanting to admit the extent of her illness, she pretended surprise at herself. Her apology hurt Ellen's heart.

"I don't know what got over me today. The drowsy spring weather, I guess. Kevin phoned from Paris, dear. I told him you weren't home yet. He'll call back at five."

At five precisely as always, the call arrived. "I'm missing you terribly," he said.

"And I you."

"What did you do today? Don't you get off earlier on Wednesdays?"

"Yes, but I took a walk afterward."

"Where did you go?"

Kevin had a habit of wanting detailed explanations for everything, which was sometimes bothersome to Ellen, but still, since he willingly gave such explanations for his activities, she really should not let it be bothersome to her.

"Went around looking into galleries."

"Did you see anything you liked?"

"Yes, for thirty-five thousand dollars."

"Well, I can't promise you anything in that range, darling. But I'll tell you, there's an art gallery in almost every fair-sized town in France, and they're not always too high priced either. Wait till you get here. You'll see a lot of landscapes, the kind you'll love. What's the weather like over there?"

"A wonderful spring afternoon, warm and soft."

"That's a perfect description of you. It's rained here all day, and it's still pouring tonight. What are you doing this very minute?"

"I was just emptying my handbag. It's full of junk."

"I was counting the minutes until five o'clock. Now I'm going to turn off the light. Big busy day tomorrow."

When she hung up, Ellen sat with the handbag on her lap, tossing things into the wastebasket: a worn-down lipstick, a torn handkerchief, a piece of a candy-bar wrapper, and a card. *Mark Sachs,* it read, under the name of the gallery.

Momentarily, she felt a tiny pang of regret. Wouldn't the young man have been astounded if she had said, "Yes, I love it, I'll take it"? She would have enjoyed seeing his face, but that was absurd. She tore up the card and tossed it, too, into the basket.

About two weeks later Ellen walked through Fifty-seventh Street carrying a pair of shoes that she had just bought. The shop windows were filled with colorful objects; adult toys, she called them, even while enjoying them. There in the gallery's window was "her" painting. Really lovely, she thought, and was wondering to herself whether, ridiculous as it was, she might try to paint something like it: a brook in falling snow, dark water, dark bare trees, the sky to be light gray, almost white—

"So you're still thinking about it?" And there was her salesman, coming through the door.

"No, I can't possibly do it. The only reason I said I'd think about it was that I wanted to make an easy exit."

He smiled. "People do that all the time. It's understandable."

"What I'm really thinking about is how I might try to paint something like it."

"You're an artist?"

"I don't dare say that. I'm a would-be artist."

"Even the greatest had to start."

There came then a pause with nothing to fill it, and she moved away from the window.

"Going east or west?" he asked.

"West to Fifth and then uptown."

"So am I."

Homecoming

They walked to the corner, waited at the red light, and turned north. She felt awkward and foolish to be keeping step with this total stranger and having nothing to say.

Mark Sachs was his name. She remembered how it had looked on the card, discreet and refined, almost like engraving.

"Nice to get through early," he said. "We're not all that busy this time of year. Nice to get some air."

"It's not too hot to walk, for a change. I'm going to get off the avenue and go through the park."

"So am I. Whenever I visit my parents on Central Park West, I like to cut through the park and out at the natural history museum. That gives me about a mile and a half's worth of exercise, anyway."

The dialogue was now slowly starting up.

"They've done wonders over at that museum. But my love is always art museums. I thought that after graduation I'd get a great job in one right away, but the great job hasn't turned up. They never tell you how hard it is to find one. So I'm working in the museum shop, which is fun, and I'm hoping it will—who knows?—lead to something."

"I took my job the same way. I knew I wanted to do something in the art world. I didn't want to be a doctor or a lawyer or a teacher. Maybe if I'd grown up in the West, I'd be a sheep rancher, I don't know. So I got an MBA with the thought that I'd eventually own an art gallery."

Some little boys were playing with toy boats at the pond. For a moment they stood watching.

"What would New York be without the park?" Ellen wondered aloud. "I played with boats right here. I actually grew up in this park. It feels like home, as if I owned it."

"Same with me, from roller skates to baseball."

"You must live right across from me. I'm near the art museum, and you're near the Natural History."

"No, I have an apartment in the Village with two friends from college. It's just my parents who live uptown. I try to visit them on Wednesdays."

"That's nice. I've been living at home since graduation last May because I—" And with a feeling that these explanations, made to a stranger, were really uncalled for, she stopped.

He looked at his watch. "Well, I'm early for dinner. They'll be surprised." Their paths were branching, yet he still was not walking away. "It's been nice talking to you."

"Yes," she said with a smile, and, looking at her own watch, remarked, "yes, early for dinner, but there's nobody home to be surprised. They're in Maine."

"So you'll prop up a book while you eat alone? That's what I like to do."

This situation was absolutely ridiculous. Two strangers having a stilted, silly dialogue instead of going along on their ways.

"No," she said, "I missed the morning paper. I'll pick one up and read it in the sandwich shop."

"A sandwich? Is that all you're going to eat?"

"Oh, they have more stuff if I want any. There's a great place on Madison. It's really much more than just a sandwich shop."

And still they stood there where the path forked. He seemed to be studying her face, then seemed about to speak, closed his mouth, and at last, did speak. "Would you mind—I mean would you mind if I went along?"

Ellen had, then, a moment of doubt. Wasn't this, when you came down to it, nothing else but a pickup? On the other hand, where was the harm? You might look at it as an hour's worth of adventure, a small, insignificant adventure, a little fun.

In front of the restaurant there were a few tables beneath an awning. When they had sat down and given their orders, they fell again into awkward silence until Ellen broke it, saying frankly, "I'm sorry I took so much of your time for nothing that day. You thought I was really going to buy it, didn't you?"

"You can always hope. And if people look— well, look as if—"

She laughed, interrupting him. "It's this ring. People see it and naturally assume things. I can't blame them, though I hate the idea of it."

"Then why do you wear it?"

"It's my engagement ring."

He seemed to be embarrassed, as if he had committed a social blunder, although, as she was well aware, it was she who had brought up the subject.

"He's working at his law firm's branch in Paris right now."

"So you'll be living in Paris."

"For a year or two. I'm hoping to learn things there that might add to my job résumé when I come back."

"I spent a year abroad while I was in college. Then I went there again for two summers and wrote an article about how architecture changed when Hausmann rebuilt the city."

"Was it published?"

"In a small, a very small, magazine. It didn't amount to much. Hardly original. But someday I'd like to do a book on how to remake a whole city, the way Hausmann did."

She asked curiously, "Do you like what you're doing now?"

"I'm saving money for that art gallery and the book I want to do, so I have to like it. In the meantime I'm learning things. I'm out in the real world meeting people. Something interesting happens every day. Sometimes sad, sometimes funny."

Her glance met his eyes, in which she was startled to see again a lovely glint of gold around the iris. It was a lively glint, and yet if you were asked, you would say his eyes were thoughtful.

"What happened today? Something funny or sad?"

"I'll tell you and you can tell me which it is. An old couple came in and walked around for a long time. They were country people, and this was their first trip to New York. He wanted to buy her a present. She said she'd like a picture to hang above the sofa. The one she liked was your snow on the brook. Good judgment. 'You like it, Mother?' he said, although quite obviously she was not his mother. And he asked the price. So I told him it was thirty-five. 'That's pretty steep,' he said, 'but since it's her birthday, she's entitled to it.' And he took out his wallet. 'Might as well pay cash.' I saw my colleague's face grow red with silent laughter. I told the man very gently that there'd been a misunderstanding, that I should have explained he'd need to add some zeros. He was astonished. 'You mean you'd charge over a thousand dollars for that? Excuse me, sir, I don't mean to be impertinent, but that's highway robbery.' The poor lady was disappointed and they went out still shaking their heads. So what do you think about that story?"

"It touches my heart. It's far more sad than funny."

"Of course it is."

For some reason the simple anecdote had moved her excessively. She had a curious awareness of sharpened senses: of the afternoon sun's painful glitter on metal, of ice cubes squirming in her glass, of a passing woman's anxious face.

"Tell me a funny one," she said.

So, as if she had given a command, he did. He was a raconteur, an entertainer. They had drunk a second tall glass of iced coffee and the sun had gone behind the buildings across the avenue before they realized that it was late.

"You're really a humorist," she told him. "You're really a wit."

"Thank you. If I have any wit at all, I get what little I have from my father. Dinnertime was fun when I was a kid. It still is. Which reminds me, I'd better run."

Ellen went home thinking about Mark Sachs. He was an interesting person, so very alive. She had a feeling that he never wasted a living moment. Then another thought fled across her mind. *What is he like when he makes love?* She felt unspeakably foolish, and, ashamed of her foolishness, crushed the thought at its birth. Who was he, anyway? She would never see him again.

Another Wednesday arrived. It was very hot, the kind of day when you think of doing nothing but being near water or, if that is not possible, of reading somewhere in the shade. The perfect spot in the park was the place where the walk forked toward the West Side. It was even breezy there, and very quiet.

From time to time, as people passed, Ellen glanced up over the book. Some boys came by on Rollerblades. Two nursemaids pushed baby carriages. An old man scattered crumbs for birds as he walked. Then suddenly, there was Mark Sachs.

He sat down beside her and looked at her book. "French. You're preparing yourself. Are you leaving pretty soon?"

"The date's not been set, but soon. He—we have to find an apartment."

"My favorite place is the Place des Vosges."

"Expensive tastes!"

"Just idle talk. What's your choice?"

"That depends on how soon and how far Kevin moves up in the firm." And suddenly, conscious of an obligation, she said loyally, "He's very bright. Someone told me he's shot up like a rocket."

"So eventually you will afford the snowy brook, or something like it."

"I told you I'm going to paint one of my own."

"Are you really any good? Seriously?"

Ellen shook her head. "I don't believe so, although once they hung something of mine in our church hall in the country."

He nodded, then said abruptly, "I'm Jewish. Orthodox. That is, my parents are."

"So? I'm an Episcopalian. What about it?"

He shrugged. "I don't know. I just like to set things straight, I suppose."

She wondered why he wanted to set things straight. . . .

Now she pursued the subject. "That sounds interesting. Tell me about yourself"—adding quickly—"if you want to."

"There's nothing much to tell."

"Oh, no. There always is. For instance, why aren't you Orthodox, like your parents?"

"Just never rubbed off on me. My father's a good man, sometimes hard to live with if you don't agree with him on certain things. He wanted me to be a surgeon too. He wanted it badly, so that's been a big disappointment to him, although he never says so anymore, so he's evidently forced himself to accept me as I am. Mother accepts things more easily." Mark smiled. "Or at least she pretends to. She's a social worker, trained to unravel the knots and make peace. Anyway, her background is very different from Dad's. She's never had to struggle, and that's a big part of the difference."

This candor touched Ellen. It was not that he had revealed anything very intimate, but rather that he had responded so easily, so confidently, to a stranger. And suddenly, without plan, words came out of her mouth.

"I waited for you here today. I remembered you said you pass here on Wednesdays."

"I thought you did," he said.

This was not making any sense. Why had she admitted such a thing? The man would think she was pursuing him. In the first place it was only half true.

"I meant," she said to correct herself, "I come here anyway. It's a favorite spot of mine. And then it crossed my mind that it would be such a funny coincidence if we were to meet here again."

He was looking at her lips, which today were coral, to match her summer dress. Then he looked up straight into her eyes. His own were smiling.

"Can we perhaps have dinner one evening?" he asked. "If that's an inappropriate question, please say so."

"Inappropriate?" she repeated.

"Yes, because you are engaged."

"I go out with friends. Kevin doesn't mind. What does a dinner mean?"

"Well then, I'll call you. But I want you to do something first. Look in the telephone book for my father's name and office address. Dr. Aaron Sachs. You will see where I come from and that I have a respectable past, at least."

"Don't you think I can see for myself that you're respectable?"

"No, I could be Jack the Ripper in a good suit. You should be more careful."

She laughed. "All right, Jack. I will be."

When he left her, she sat looking after him. At the turn in the path he looked back at her, did not wave, and went on.

The sun had gone in and the air was sultry. It was an effort to lift her feet as she walked home. And a heavy tiredness overcame her. At home on the answering machine there was a message from her father.

"Your mother's not feeling well. It's nothing acute, but we both think she'll be better off at home. We're driving back tomorrow."

The subliminal message was clear: her mother's time was approaching. It had been long in coming and was no longer a shock, but perhaps a mercy. And yet, when she passed her mother's photograph on the piano, she had to turn away.

The telephone rang, making an alien noise in the silent room. "Where've you been?" Kevin asked. "I've made three tries in the last hour."

"In the park, reading."

"Poor girl. I know it's an awfully lonely time for you."

"Well, I have the job, and I read a lot." There seemed to be nothing else to say.

"You sound so distant, Ellen. What is it?"

"Mom's troubles have come back. Dad's bringing her home tomorrow."

"Oh, Lord, I'm sorry. But you knew that it was coming. You'll be brave. I'll help you any way I can."

"I know you will, Kevin."

"Now I have a bit of good news for you. I'm coming home for Thanksgiving, and I'll be in the U.S. for two months, so we can be married and return to France together about the first of February."

"Yes, but if something happens to Mom?"

"We'll plan a quiet wedding whatever way things go. Just the family. Very simple. Actually, I like that better than a lot of fuss."

When they hung up, she began to cry. It wasn't only because of Mom. What was it? It was confusion. It was everything.

Mark and Ellen had dinner together. They went to a concert in the park, and then to another. One rainy night they saw a movie, took a taxi to her door, and talked very seriously all the way about the movie. He seemed to have lost his humor and wit.

Her father was cheerful when she came in. Everybody was cheerful in Mom's presence these days.

"How was the picture?"

"Interesting. Very well done, I thought."

"Did your friend like it? Your friend—what's her name again?"

"Fran. She was in my class."

"Kevin phoned," her mother said. "I think he was a little annoyed when I told him you had gone to the movies. He had told you to expect his call."

"Oh, I'm sorry! I must have misunderstood." But she had not misunderstood; she had forgotten.

After her father left the room, her mother asked a strange question. "Are you happy, Ellen?"

"I'm fine, Mom. Or almost fine. I'll be really perfect when I see you feeling better again."

Her mother smiled faintly and was silent.

She went to her room and got ready for bed.

When she had removed her ring, she laid it on the night table and stood looking at it. Her heart seemed to be shaking in her chest.

One day her mother said, "Our dentist saw you at the concert with a young man."

"Really? Yes, I was there with one of the women at the shop and her boyfriend. The three of us."

By October it was almost too chilly to meet in the park. When Mark came uptown on a Sunday afternoon, he was prepared with a heavy sweater and heavy shoes for a walk in the woods. Ellen was dressed the same way. This was the first time they had seen each other wearing anything but office clothes.

"You look so different," she cried.

"And so do you. More real. No, that's not quite what I meant. More natural, maybe? Except for the ring."

She flexed her hand and stared at it, saying slowly, "It's very beautiful . . . but I'd just as soon not have it."

"Then why have it?"

Belva Plain

"Things happen. Sometimes you don't know why they happen."

He was looking over her shoulder into the trees when he spoke. "Your parents like him."

"Very much."

"It isn't fair for you to be here." And when she failed to answer, he said angrily, "If I were engaged to marry a girl, I wouldn't want to know that she was meeting another man this Sunday afternoon in Central Park."

She only looked at him.

"Come here," he said, pulling her by the arm.

In the thicket that might have been miles away instead of a mere few yards from Fifth Avenue, they had their first kiss, a kiss that did not want to end.

"Oh, God," she said. "Oh, God." And cried.

They had to go somewhere, so the following week Mark took a room in a luxurious hotel, where, like any pair of tourists, they entered with their luggage.

"It's too expensive," Ellen protested. "You can't afford it."

"No, we deserve a beautiful place. You," he

136

said, "you. I would die for you. Do you know that?"

They lay awake in each other's arms, not wanting to sleep, not wanting the night to end.

"God, I love you," he said.

There were tears in his eyes. Kevin had never been so moved, nor had she. This love and this lovemaking were entirely new. Different people, she thought, and I never had any idea how different it might be. How could I have known? This man is like me in every way. We are the same.

Each week they changed hotels, and Ellen made excuses for her nights away from home.

"This won't do," Mark said. "I should go to your house and tell the truth."

"You can't do that. I'm still engaged. Anyway, my mother's too sick to go through what she'd have to go through with Dad. And what of your people? Will your father tear his clothes when he hears this? I've heard that they do."

"No," Mark said grimly, "but he'll feel like doing it."

"We couldn't help it, could we? When you're growing up, you always ask how people can tell whether it's the real thing or not. And no one is ever able to give you a satisfying answer. 'Oh, you'll know,' is all they say. But it's true. You do know."

On the first of November the shops put pumpkins on display, real ones, or chocolate, or paper. And Mark commented as they were walking that Thanksgiving was around the corner.

"Yes, I can't sleep for dreading it."

That evening her mother asked again, "Are you happy, Ellen?"

"You've asked me that before," she said gently.

"You wouldn't tell me if you weren't."

That's right, I wouldn't, Ellen thought. These are your last weeks, the doctors warned, perhaps your last days. I wonder whether you know it. If you do, you don't tell us either. We all want to spare one another.

When Susan died, Kevin flew home for the funeral. Afterward and for the next few days the house was besieged with visitors and telephone calls. Toward the end of that hard week Kevin decided that Ellen needed some respite and must come with him to his apartment for a few hours' peace.

She thought, as he turned the key in the lock, that this was going to be the worst hour of her life. Often as she had rehearsed this scene in every possible variation, she had still no clear idea of what she could possibly tell him that would not hurt him too much.

When he put his arms around her, she did not resist, but stood stiffly with her own arms at her sides. She had clearly intended to be very, very kind, yet it had suddenly become impossible for her to respond to the pressure of his body.

Drawing a step back and with a puzzled, anxious frown, he said, "I don't understand. Aren't you happy to see me?"

"Yes, but—but there's been so much," she stammered. "It's so hard for me to talk, I—"

"I know. Your mother," he said gently.

There was a choking lump in her throat. Her glance went toward the window, toward black night and a scattering of lights.

"Not only that. I—oh, Kevin, I don't know how to say it. I feel like a thief, a betrayer, a liar. . . . This is nothing I ever dreamed would happen. But it did. It just did. I never wanted—"

He was staring at her. She saw him reach out

and hold onto the back of a chair. And for a few moments they both stood facing each other in disbelief.

"Who is he, Ellen?"

"It doesn't matter, does it?" she pleaded.

"I'm not going to kill him. Tell me."

"I met him one day this summer. He's a decent, good man, as you are. Neither one of us wanted to deceive or to hurt. We couldn't help it. That's the truth, the whole truth, I swear."

"And of course you have been sleeping with him while I was away, missing you."

She saw his hand grip the chair. White knuckles, that was the expression, and they really were white.

"I could call you names. I could say plenty of things, but I won't. You aren't worth the effort."

Now, so many years later, that scene was still alive, its colors, its sounds and silence, still fresh, that scene and the others that followed it.

Kevin went back to France with the ring in his pocket. Through mutual friends she learned that he had taken the break very hard, yet no harder than her father had done.

"Where's truth and honor, Ellen? My daughter, hiding away, lying, cheating on a good man. It's an incredible outrage."

"If you would only see Mark. It's not fair to condemn without seeing him," she said, not pleading, but with effort keeping her head high.

"I know enough without seeing him. You don't belong with him. That's all. For your own good I've asked you to reconsider, and you won't. You are a fool, a willful little fool, and I have no more to say to you."

The same drama had been played out at Mark's house. So Ellen packed her belongings, left a loving note for her father, and married Mark at City Hall.

Eventually, they all had to meet. It was Gran who, more than half a year later, had engineered the meeting in the guise of a wedding reception. A few elderly relatives and some of Gran's neighbors had been the buffers on the great lawn, which was so great that certain people—the two fathers—needed to have no contact with each other.

"Contact at glaring distance," Mark said.

Despite the summer day, the roses and garden party punch, it had been really horrible. Only the elderly ladies, enthralled by the Romeo-and-Juliet occasion, had valiantly kept the conversational balloon from leaking all its air and shriveling onto the ground.

Brenda had been the first to soften, and for that Ellen would thank her forever. It was the birth of Lucy that finally had softened the two fathers enough to accept the marriage as long as they never had to see each other.

By this time, Ellen thought as she put the ironing board away and got ready for dinner, the hatred can only be called pathological. Well, so be it, she was thinking when Mark came in.

"I'm starved," he said after he had put his briefcase down, kissed first Ellen and then the children. "What's this here?"

"An invitation from Gran. She wants us to come up next week and stay overnight."

Mark read aloud, *"Don't mention this to your father, Ellen. I'm inviting Mark's parents too. Next time it will be your father's turn."*

"Are my parents going?" he asked.

"Yes, we're to ride up together."

"We really should see your gran more often.

She's a sweet old soul. I always think she must have been like you when she was young."

"When Freddie is just a bit older, it will be easier and we'll do it."

"Remember that wedding reception? What an ordeal! I came home in a sweat because of those two men. Nine years ago! I'll tell you right now, I couldn't go through it again." And he laughed at the recollection.

Chapter 7

*A*nnette had a habit that had taken root as long ago as her childhood. It was her custom, no matter what might have occurred during the day, to look ahead each night before falling asleep to something happy in the next day. More often than not the something was simple, such as a trip to browse in the local bookstore, or an afternoon with an old friend. It might even be something quite trivial, like having pancakes and sausage for breakfast on a winter morning. Small comforts, she often thought, do help to soften large griefs, no matter what anyone says. Not, she would mentally add, that I am any great au-

145

thority on grief. I have had very few of them: my husband's death, and the deaths of poor Cynthia's twins.

This present sorrow could not possibly compare with those. Nevertheless, the breach between her sons had gone on far too long, and it hurt. Consider all those expressions fixed in the language, like *blood brothers,* and *brotherly love;* those two men were too old and too intelligent to cast such precious bonds away.

Then there were other things that offended her sense of rightness: the impending and, in her opinion, entirely unnecessary divorce between Cynthia and her nice young husband was one. The in-laws' feud that burdened Ellen's household was another. What on earth was happening to people who should know better? Why couldn't they just behave themselves like adults? Act your age! she wanted to say to them.

But that was not so easy. In a brief, inspired moment she had believed it might be, and so had written those tricky invitations. Now, tomorrow morning, her chickens would be coming home to roost. And she was scared to death.

She stood now in the library, talking to the

portrait of Lewis. His keen brown eyes paid attention; on his left hand, resting upon an open book, the wedding band gleamed. For a moment she had an old, familiar impression that he was teasing her: *Oh, Annette, what a meddler and busybody you are.*

"No, I'm not," she replied aloud. "If you were still here, you yourself would give your sons what-for."

Two boys who played in the bathtub together. And she almost had to laugh at the memory of the day when, half grown and old enough to bathe themselves, they had let the water overflow.

Loud shrieks, as glee turned into rage, had brought both parents running. A small lake was forming on the floor while the boys wrestled in the tub.

"He got soap in my eyes!"

"He punched me!"

By the time the slippery, protesting pair had been lifted out and pacified, by the time the floor had been mopped and order restored, both Lewis and she had been almost as wet as the boys. And how had it ended? They had all gone out for ice cream, as sweetly and happily as you please.

If only today's troubles could be so easily tidied away!

Cynthia. All these tragic divorces, instead of putting some effort into marriage.

"It wasn't all champagne and roses for us, was it, Lewis? And then those kids Ellen and Mark. Were they supposed to fall in love to please their parents? We didn't. You didn't have a bean when we were married, and I know my parents weren't delighted about it, either, but they never said so."

When Annette's voice ceased, the room was too quiet. The dogs in their baskets slept deeply, without twitching in dreams of the hunt. The sleep of the old, she thought. They're old like me. I hope they won't outlive me, for who will take care of them? I wish I knew how long I have, so I could make plans. People do live into their nineties these days, though. Still, you can't count on it. It seems as if you can't count on anything, although I suppose it's age that makes me take that point of view. Age that makes me want to lecture to the young. And yet, I'm afraid of them. What kind of a mess are we going to have here tomorrow?

It was then, as she sat down in front of the

telephone, that she knew she must ask for help. To do otherwise was nothing but foolhardy.

Marian Lester lived halfway between the Byrne house and the high school, where she taught. Only in her late forties and looking ten years younger, she was an unusual person to be a friend of Annette Byrne. But Annette had been active in community affairs, even on the board of education for many years after her grandchildren, let alone her children, were grown. And so they had had a long acquaintanceship. Then suddenly a friendship had begun.

One Saturday morning Annette had been surprised to see Marian in the group of kindergarten children who were having their nature walk through Byrnes' woods.

"Don't tell me you're tired of teaching teen-agers," she said.

"No way. But I'm on the board of our local wildlife committee, and they ran short of helpers for this morning's outing. So here I am, filling in. It's rather fun for a change."

Marian looked wistful, Annette thought. She had been a widow for several years and lived alone, her children being adults and far away.

The little town was hardly overfull of desirable single men, and anyway schoolteachers had scant time to go out searching. Such a pretty woman too! It was a waste. . . .

On impulse Annette suggested dinner.

"That is, if you have nothing better to do one night this week," she said, with tact. "I know an old lady isn't the most exciting company."

Marian smiled. "That depends on who she is. And you don't have to specify midweek. I'm not often busy on weekends either."

"Then what about tonight?"

"I'd love it, thank you."

They had a very pleasant evening, the first of many. They were both bookworms, music lovers, and nature lovers. They were passionate about causes. Like all women who are mothers, they had their own stories to relate.

Annette had the advantage of means that had enabled her to travel the world, yet she seldom talked about the things she had seen.

"I always say that the worst bores are people with travel tales about their hotel bargains and sick stomachs."

"You never bore me. I *want* to hear about the

Ganges. Do you really see floating bodies? Did they serve fermented mare's milk in Mongolia? No, you never bore me."

There was an unusual serenity about Marian. At least, it seemed outwardly to be so. What was within, of course, one could not know. The thoughtful, listening expression and calm voice, even the smooth curve of the dark hair from the center parting to the ears, were all soothing to hear and look at. It seemed to Annette that Marian must never have had any of both Cynthia's and Ellen's busyness—inherited, most probably, from me, she would think with a grin.

So they admired each other, and exchanged the small favors that friends do. Marian knitted a handsome sweater for Annette, while Annette gave books and a matinee in the city. And they confided things, as friends do.

Therefore Marian knew all about the tangled quarrels in Annette's extended family. Therefore Annette was now at the telephone.

"I need your help, you see. I want to have things straightened out. It's ridiculous for these people to waste life like this." And then, as a doubt rose, she asked, "Tell me the truth. Am I wrong, Marian? Am I sticking my nose into other people's business?"

"Well, of course you are, but that doesn't mean you shouldn't do it. Some of the best things in the world happen because people stick their noses in."

"So you'll come? You can sit comfortably in the snuggery—that's my little office where I pay bills and read mail—you can read there. Then if you hear any loud argument, and I'm sure you will, come out and be a buffer."

"I'll be there early. It sounds interesting."

Hearing the smile in Marian's voice, Annette felt her dread recede. At least she would have an ally.

"Go to sleep, Annette, and think of something nice for tomorrow, the way you always do."

Promptly at ten o'clock Gene's tires crunched over the gravel drive. From his earliest years when he had first learned to tell time, he had always been either right on the dot or else five minutes early. His reliability had been a family byword ever since his childhood. Perhaps, Annette thought, this time will be different and I shall be able to reach that strong sense of what is required and right.

Coffee and his favorite cinnamon rolls were set on a tray in the sunroom, where he liked to sit on a wicker garden chair among flowering plants.

"You've had the chairs painted," he observed the minute he walked in.

"I thought white would be a nice change. Do you like it?"

"Very nice. You've never lost your touch with African violets, I see. It looks like summer in here."

"The light's good. That's all you need, no particular skill."

"You'd never think it was twenty-five degrees above outside."

"I got a feel of it when I let the dogs out."

"Old Roscoe keeps going, doesn't he?"

"Yes, he's in fine shape for his age. Look at him. He loves the sun."

Gene looked at the dog, who was bathing in a pool of heat beside Annette's chair. He looked at his mother, who was also in fine shape for her age, slender and beautifully groomed, from polished shoes and pale blue country woolens to wavy white hair. Then he looked at the tray with its two cups and two pl es. So she was not expecting anyone to join them, he reasoned, and was relieved of his earlier vision of doctors or lawyers come to discuss alarming news.

"I've been rummaging around in the attic," she said. "It's amazing how things accumulate almost before you know it. And I found some surprises. You know, I thought we'd given your trains away years ago, but here they are, in perfect condition, each piece wrapped in tissue paper. Your father must have done it. There's a huge layout—do you remember?—bridges, tunnels, a river, villages, and trees. It will be a real treasure for Freddie in a couple of years."

"It certainly will be," Gene agreed, although where they would put the huge layout in that place where they were living was surely a puzzle.

He wondered about this conversation, too, and why he had been invited just today. Invited? Was not *summoned* perhaps a better word? For the letter, when he thought about it, was in a way rather strange. Again, why just today? And be prepared, if possible, to stay overnight? It would have seemed more natural if she had said, *I'd love to have a visit from you soon. How about next week or the week after?*

On the other hand, there was probably nothing to it at all except a normal desire, very normal at her age, to be with her son very soon.

"And how's Lucy? I haven't seen her since Labor Day weekend, and I miss her."

"She's an absolute joy. I took her to see the *Nutcracker* last week. The place was packed with children, but even so, I saw people looking at her and making comments. She had on a black velvet dress that Ellen said you gave her, and with that blond hair and all her chatter—"

Annette laughed. "You're nothing but a proud grandfather."

"I'll admit that. But she really does attract attention. She's the image of Ellen, don't you think? And Ellen looks a lot like you."

"Undeserved credit. Ellen looks just like her mother."

Susan. Sometimes he went for days in quiet acceptance of his loss, and sometimes the very mention of her name, a face, or a fraction of song were enough to send a thrust of pain through his chest.

And he could not help but say, "I miss her terribly."

"I know. It comes at moments, doesn't it? Like a jab in the heart."

Neither one of them spoke. She was gazing into the space above his head. She's remembering my father, Gene thought, and felt her sadness.

"Yes, yes," she said, "you look back and back. . . . It's like looking in a telescope, seeing things recede, the front lawn, the meadow, the hill, the mountain, and beyond that, each smaller and smaller the farther out you can see. As in one's life . . . things that happened long ago get smaller and smaller too."

He became alert. Annette was not given to philosophical platitudes. But since she was evidently not finished, he listened politely.

"There's another thing about time, another aspect. It's unfortunate, really quite sad, that more often the good things, when you're looking back through the years, seem to melt into a vague, rosy blur. It's the bad things that stand out like black stains. Have you noticed? I had a bad argument with my sister once, and even though we made it up, when she died, I remembered it. I didn't want to remember it, but there it was. And I was so thankful that we had made up."

So that was it, the old business again. He reached over to pour a second cup of coffee and was trying to think of an inoffensive way to keep his mother from continuing the painful subject, when Roscoe jumped up and barked. From the front hall sounded the spaniels' hysterical yapping. Then there were voices.

"Jenny, how are you?"

Oh, my God, that was Lewis!

"Jenny, you look wonderful. You never get old."

That was Daisy, dear sister-in-law with the phony English accent.

"I'll hang up your coats. Go on in. Your mother's in the sunroom."

That was Jenny, undoubtedly in on this business and bursting with curiosity.

There were three of them, including Cynthia, at the doorway looking in. Gene half rose from his chair and sank back. There was a total shocked silence; even Annette, who had risen all the way, seemed for an instant unable to move.

You've gone too far, he thought instantly. Now

that you've done it, you don't know how to handle it. Poor Mother. And pity surged in his chest.

Of course it was clear now why she had been so definite about ten o'clock. She had wanted to make sure that the cars might not pass each other on the narrow country road and have a reason to turn back.

Annette collected herself admirably. As if this were any ordinary arrival, she greeted, kissed, offered chairs, and suggested fresh coffee. But still no one moved.

Lewis spoke first. "What is this, Mother? Is this your idea of a joke? It's a very bad one, if that's what it's meant to be."

"Not at all. Plainly and simply, I wanted to see my sons together." Her heart was trembling, but her voice was steady.

"With all respect," said Daisy, "this was a very bad idea. Lewis and I have come all the way from Washington. We've been worried. Frankly, we thought you were ill."

"Does a person have to be ill to deserve a visit from you?"

"Of course not. But you have made a dreadful mistake."

"Let the men speak for themselves, please."

There they were, the brothers, not looking at each other, not saying anything, just standing there ready to flee. They were handsome men, much alike in their dignity, their dark hair slightly silvered at the temples, as if they were playing the role of distinguished citizens in an advertisement for an investment bank. Their heavy eyebrows, straight and thick, and their rather sensitive, expressive lips were like their father's. Handsome men, but still not as handsome as their father, Annette thought loyally. He would have a few thoughts for them if he were here. If they think I'm going to let them leave this room, they have another think coming. . . .

"A dreadful mistake," repeated Daisy. "I'm sorry to say so, Mother. It hurts me."

Annette was angry. Daisy was making her more angry, with her frosty courtesy. A long time ago she had spent a year at an English boarding school and had never gotten over it, in her kilts with the safety pins and her make-believe accent. You tried to like her and mostly you did like her well enough, but there had been times when you didn't, and this was one of them.

"And I'm sorry you feel that way, Daisy. But I am their mother, and I want peace between them."

Then Lewis spoke up again. "It's too late."

"Nothing's ever too late while you're still alive."

"Water over the dam, Mother."

"That's ridiculous." She was surprising herself by being able to talk straight and stand straight, while her heart was performing so madly.

"Ridiculous?" Gene repeated. "I don't know how you can say that." The last time he had seen Lewis, they were leaving the courthouse with their lawyers. They were not speaking then and would certainly not speak now. At any rate, he thought, not after what I've been through. "When people testify against each other in a courtroom, it is hardly a laughing matter."

"You're right, Gene. I withdraw the word. *Tragic* is the right one."

"Oh, please," said Cynthia, addressing nobody in particular.

She was pitiful. Gene wanted to catch his niece's eye to show, although she already must know it, that this feud with her father had nothing to do with her. But she was looking down; her face was shadowed, and terribly thin. Her fashionable suit—so unlike Ellen's conservative choices—seemed only to emphasize the change in her. He had seldom seen her since her unspeakable tragedy and then only on those few occasions when they happened to be visiting Ellen at the same time. He supposed that her visits to Ellen were rare because they were too painful. Freddie was almost as old as those twins were when—

"Come, Cynthia," Daisy commanded. "You don't need this on top of everything else."

When they left, Annette stood barring the door. "Now I ask you two to listen to me. You owe me that much. Please sit down."

"Out of love for you, I will sit," said Lewis. "I don't want to upset you any more than you already are, but—please, Mother, this is very painful, very unfair. Surely you can't have forgotten what I've been through! Between lawyers and newspaper reporters, I've had more than a fair share of misery. I've been pilloried. Must I go over it all again this morning?"

"You're missing the whole point," Annette replied softly. "What I'm asking you both to do is to put all that away. It was a—a disease. Yes, a time of sickness and suffering. Would you want, if you had been sick in the hospital, to keep reliving those weeks for the rest of your life? Wouldn't you rather try to forget about them?"

"That's exactly what I've been doing. That's exactly why Daisy and I moved to Washington, where I'm working on something very worthwhile, I hope, for the general good. So I am already putting it all behind me."

"You can't have put it all behind you while you're still estranged from your brother."

"Oh, but I can! That's been my cure. Are you asking me to forgive and forget what he did to me?" Sharp, sarcastic lawyers had shamed him, portraying him as a culprit, a careless incompetent who had not bothered to investigate a serious complaint, indifferent to the possibility of the terrible consequences that had indeed occurred and would torment his dreams forever. Indifferent? Hardly. But Gene had not helped. "Am I supposed to forget the guilt he heaped on my head? It haunts me. I didn't deserve to be torn to shreds by lawyers and reporters."

"The newspapers came to me, too, after you sent them."

Lewis's voice rose hoarsely. "I sent them? That's idiotic."

From his chair, which was as far from Lewis's chair as was possible, Gene retorted, "It's very simple. You didn't like it when I told the truth about your refusal to check on Sprague after what Victor had reported. Very simple."

"You could have toned down your remarks instead of making me look like a deliberate criminal."

What could I have toned down? Gene thought. Victor had laid the facts out on the table, and I was under oath. I should have followed up on Sprague myself right at the beginning. But I always deferred to Lewis because he was the elder who'd been in the business three years before I was.

Fresh anger flared, and Gene cried out, "You expected me to lie for you, did you? Oh, it was only a little matter of truth—"

"And honor," Lewis finished for him. Honor, from the man who had put his own daughter through hell when she dropped the man he wanted for her and made another choice.

It was all so ugly. And so terrible, coming to a head here in their mother's house. They might as well be thrusting a knife into her.

"Those poor innocents who died," Gene said. "And all you think of is yourself, how you suffered—"

"You make me sick. You're like all these high-sounding talkers whose hearts bleed easy tears for the world, while at home, with your own daughter, you—"

Gene lurched forward in the chair. "Damn you! What has Ellen got to do with all this? You don't know what you're talking about. Leave her out of it, understand?"

Flinging out his arm in his agitation, he knocked the fruit bowl off the table. It shattered to slivers, while apples and tangerines rolled away on the floor.

"Oh, I'm sorry! Sorry!" he cried, stooping to pick up the mess. "I'll buy you another bowl. Watch the broken glass, you'll cut yourself."

It was not glass; it was crystal, Lalique, to be exact, and Annette's favorite, with its delicate birds perched around the rim. They had bought it on their twenty-fifth anniversary, when they had gone abroad on the S.S. *France,* and this was the memento of those lovely days.

"Never mind," she said. "We'll clean it up later. It's nothing. No, really," she repeated, for he, the meticulous, considerate Gene, was red with embarrassment.

"I need to get out of here. Let me get some newspapers and take it off the floor before somebody gets cut." Then, "I'm sorry, Mother, but let me go home. I'll see you another time. Next week positively."

If she did not catch them both now, she never would. Of that, Annette was certain.

"No," she said harshly. "No. You are two grown men, and I can't believe that you want to behave like children. If your father were here—" She stopped, feeling the sting in the back of her nose that always preceded the gathering of tears.

"I'm glad for his sake that he isn't," Lewis said sadly.

"But I'm here! So for my sake, can't you—" she began.

"Mother, try to understand. We've lived

through disaster. It broke us. You might as well try to put the pieces of that bowl together as to do what you want us to do. Mother, it can't be done, and the sooner you recognize it, the easier it will be for you."

She saw them again—so often did the same images recur—in the bathtub together, and dressed on Sundays in matching sailor suits, and wearing mortarboards at their college commencements. She saw them, too, as they must have looked on the terrible night when the hotel crumbled apart.

Why did it matter so much that these men in late middle age were at loggerheads? She did not have any good explanation for why it mattered so much to her. It simply did. Perhaps it was just that life was so short.

"Hate," Lewis said, "takes a lot of energy, and I need all my energy now to help my daughter. Nothing else can be as important to me except you, Mother. Certainly not my brother. Now if you'll excuse me, please, I'll go find my family."

"Good riddance," Gene said when the door closed. He had put the fruit on the tray and was picking up shards with a paper napkin. "That's about the only thing he said that I can agree with."

"Beautiful! A beautiful, worthy sentiment. God help me, could I ever have dreamed I'd live to hear it?"

"Mother." He held her shoulders and spoke softly. "I know what this must do to you. I never thought I'd live through anything like it either. But it can't be helped. It's too deep and has lasted too long. And you still have each of us whenever you want us, you know that. Only, not at the same time, that's all."

Annette searched Gene's decent, intelligent face and shook her head. "I'm ashamed of you," she said in her bitterness, "ashamed, do you hear? And you both ought to be ashamed of yourselves."

Then she wrenched herself free of his hands and went out.

In the meantime Daisy and Cynthia were in the library. Daisy was seething.

"I can't get over your grandmother. Of all people, so tactful, so Old World, really, to do a thing like this. God knows whether those two men will come to blows in there—I don't mean that—or maybe, who knows, maybe I do. They could. Anything can happen. In this world we have to be prepared for any crazy thing."

"Yes," said Cynthia, a trifle sharply, as one who should know very well about that.

She was at the window, staring out at gloom, wintry land, frozen pond, and lowering, dark sky. "It looks like snow or sleet or something."

"Oh, great. I'd like to get back to the city before it starts. I hate driving on ice. Stop twisting your necklace; you'll break it."

"If it wants to break, let it."

Daisy scolded herself: Here I talk about a necklace, when it's her heart that's broken. From having had everything, she has nothing. It's like being bombed, or burnt out, or beaten to death. Damn Andrew for giving her this last blow. Damn him to the ends of the earth. If only there were something we could do for her. We talk and talk, Lewis and I. We think and try to imagine a miracle, of walking in and finding her standing calmly again, in that quiet way of hers, with that touch of a smile at the corners of her mouth.

It had been a bad idea to bring her here today.

This old town had too many memories, the church, the wedding, and the party in this house when they came back from the honeymoon, she coming down the stairs in her lavender dress . . . And then, the cemetery.

"This is a beautiful room," she observed. "When your father's finished in Washington and we're home again, I think I'll redo our den in these colors. Annette won't mind if I copy her, I'm sure."

"Mom, I'm all right." Cynthia spoke without turning from the window. "You don't have to work so hard to cheer me up."

"It's not hard work. It comes naturally, darling. And you do seem to need cheering up."

"I know I'm dull company. I shouldn't have come. I'm better off working. At least I'm helping people, and that helps me."

"Well, that's true." Daisy, hesitating over a question, decided to proceed with it and ask whether there was anything new happening, any word of Andrew.

"Wouldn't I tell you if there were?"

"I should think his parents would try to get in touch with you. After all—"

"I suppose they've given up. You and Dad haven't gotten in touch with Andrew either."

"I wouldn't care to be there when your father meets him."

"As far as I can see, he never will, so you needn't worry."

Sometimes, when she was unable to fall asleep and lay still counting her heartbeats, Cynthia's thoughts churned, inventing situations in which she would have to confront Andrew: on the street, in a bus where he would take the seat next to hers and try to argue her into letting him come back, or at the theater where he would be sitting directly behind her and she, feeling his eyes on the back of her head, would be waiting for some vengeful, humiliating move or words from him. And as she imagined that scene, her muscles would tense in dread.

Perhaps, inevitably, she would have to see him in the divorce court. She had no idea whether the parties did have to meet there. If they did, she would act as if he were invisible.

The pond was dark blue. Out in the center beyond the ice, two swans and their young were swimming, their young now, in December, having grown to be as large as the parents. This was the time of year when, like little birds being driven out of the nest and made to fly, the cygnets were to be sent forth into the world. And Cynthia, who had known about swans ever since her grandfather had raised the first pair, wondered how many generations this present family was removed from that first. She watched now as the big one, the father, rose into the air, flew low and returned to his huddled family, rose again, and repeated the flight. He was teaching them how to fly.

Swans were monogamous, faithful.

Then, as she turned her head to follow the great white wings, she saw a car come up the driveway. Now who? Who else was coming? Surely not Mark and Ellen?

"Oh, no! Mom, you won't believe this. Come look, it's Ellen with Mark and the children and, yes, they've got his father and mother with them too."

Daisy peered out. "Of all the senseless, confused, and idiotic messes, this gets the first place. What can have possessed Annette? If I didn't know she wasn't, I'd say she must be senile."

"Do you realize that those two fathers despise each other? They haven't been in the same room for the last—it must be eight or nine years!"

There was a slight bustle in the hall, and then a short procession, with Jenny at the head, appeared around the corner and paused for a moment of astonished recognition.

Jenny was in a red-faced fluster. "You'll all be comfortable in here. There are plenty of chairs. Can I get you anything?"

"I think we have everything. Thank you, Jenny," Ellen replied.

Indeed, they seemed to be laden; they had a tote bag full of toys, a diaper bag, and an armful of sweaters. Mark held a partially consumed bottle in one hand, while with the other he juggled Freddie onto his knee.

Now Gene has two enemies, Daisy thought. This should be interesting.

"This is quite a surprise," Mark said brightly. "We were wondering whose car that might be."

"We rented it," Daisy said.

"Do you remember each other?" asked Ellen. "My aunt, Daisy Byrne, and Mark's parents, Aaron and Brenda Sachs. Dr. Sachs."

"How do you do?" said Daisy, who only remembered black whiskers.

Lucy had run to Brenda and was being hugged. "Grandma's little doll. Somebody loves Grandma and Grandma loves somebody."

"Where's Gran?" asked Lucy.

The question floated for a moment until Daisy replied, "She's in the sunroom with Gene and Lewis."

Ellen gasped. "What's happening? Is it working out?"

"I doubt it. Personally, when I left there, I was thankful that neither of them is armed."

"Oh, what can Gran have been thinking of?"

"Only Gran can answer that, I'm afraid."

"It's all so sad and so unnecessary," Cynthia said.

Ellen smiled at her. Regardless of their fathers they were fond of each other. But their paths had led them far apart. It must be agonizing for her to see me with my children, she thought. I understand why she doesn't visit.

"I think Freddie's wet," Mark said.

"What, again? Stick your hand in and feel."

"No, my mistake. I apologize, Freddie. Now get down and play with your blocks."

He's a sweet man, Cynthia thought. She watched the blocks tumble into a little pile on the floor. She hadn't seen Freddie in months, which was wrong of her. It made her sorry and ashamed to think that she, living in the same city, had been staying away. She could have come to the party when he turned one. Sending a good present was not the same. He was a cute little boy, still pudgy, like a baby.

"Do you live nearby?" asked Brenda, who, having caught Daisy's eye, felt it necessary to say something to her.

"No, we're in Washington now."

Brenda nodded. "I thought I remembered Ellen's mentioning that you had moved out of New York, but I didn't recall where to."

She was making conversation. It's like being at a funeral, waiting for the service to begin; you always feel that you have to make some remark to the stranger who's sitting next to you. What an odd thought to be having, Brenda said to herself, and looked toward Aaron for solidarity.

But Aaron had gone down on his knees beside

Freddie and the blocks. He was feeling signals in the room. They seemed to stream like electric currents speeding through the world, filling the air with messages from man to man. He sensed the vibrations in this room. Brenda was feeling out of place; his son was uneasy; that young woman—Cynthia, wasn't that her name?—was grieving; and her mother was suppressing a boiling anger.

Ah, stop it, he admonished himself. None of this concerns you.

Lucy asked Brenda, "Is Papa Gene here?"

Brenda's glance consulted Mark, who did not see the glance because he was, in like silent fashion, consulting Ellen.

"I don't know," replied Brenda.

Lucy slid down from her lap and went to Daisy. "You said he was here with Gran. Why doesn't he come to see me?"

"I don't know," Daisy said.

"I want to see him."

"Well, you can't right now."

Spoiled, thought Daisy. When a child's that pretty, it gets too much attention. And she really did have a doll's face. You couldn't help wondering how Laura would have looked at this age. You wonder too much, she told herself.

"You have to wait," Ellen said.

"But I want to see him," insisted Lucy.

"Not now, Lucy." And without thinking Ellen explained to Daisy, "She really loves my father so much."

"Apparently so," Daisy said. The child was appealing, but she was in no mood to cater to any child, however appealing. And what a stupid remark for Ellen to make, to her of all people.

Ellen was restless. When to the room at large she remarked, "I wonder whether they plan to stay in there all day," no one answered.

Aaron built a tower of blocks, which Freddie, with great glee, overturned. He kept building more until Freddie lost interest and began to forage in the bag of toys for something else, whereupon he got up, brushed off his trousers, and looked out of the window, observing that the sky was threatening.

"It's a good thing we're staying overnight," Mark said. "I wouldn't want to be on the roads with the kids if it should get as bad as it looks."

"Are you invited for overnight?" Ellen asked Cynthia.

"We—" Cynthia started to say, when Daisy interrupted.

"We were supposed to, but we are definitely not going to. As a matter of fact, I'm ready to start right now."

"Don't you like Gran's house?" asked Lucy, turning wide blue eyes up at Daisy. "Don't you like Gran?"

Daisy liked children, but at the moment this one was really a bit much. Her parents, considering the situation, should make her keep quiet. They should see that we are all nerves here.

Lucy was still surveying Daisy from top to toe. Apparently, she was fascinated by Daisy. "You have flowers on your shirt," she observed.

"I do."

"They're pretty."

"Thank you."

"Why does that man hate Papa Gene?"

This child was too smart. And why, Daisy wondered, must she fasten on me?

"I don't know. I don't know anything about it," she countered, giving Lucy the smile that often, but not always, can placate a persistent child.

"You do know. You said the man in the sun-room."

The adults looked from one to another. *Did you ever? You have to watch everything you say in front of them.*

"Grandpa," asked Lucy, losing interest in Daisy, "you don't hate Papa Gene, do you?"

Suddenly, Aaron had a coughing fit. And Mark said hastily, "Come, Lucy. Come over and take a toy out of your bag and play."

"They're all baby toys, Daddy. I don't like any of them."

"You're being awfully stubborn," he said impatiently.

Brenda corrected her son. "Mark, anybody can see she's bored. She's only six. What do you expect?"

She would, Daisy thought. A social worker, I heard. Overindulgent. Crammed with pop-Freudian psychology. Just tell the child to be quiet. My head is splitting.

The message came clearly to Aaron: She doesn't approve of Brenda. Country-club Republican. Captain of girls' hockey in school. Champion golfer. Champion hang-glider, for all I know. God, I'd like to get out of this place. Can't breathe in this atmosphere.

"What on earth is going on in there?" Daisy cried.

"They'll have to be out soon," Ellen soothed. "I'm sure everything will be all right."

You think so, Cynthia thought not unkindly, because everything turned out all right for you.

"That Gene," Daisy began to protest. "There's never any telling what that man—" and stopped.

"You're forgetting yourself, Mom," Cynthia told her. "He's Ellen's father."

"I'm sorry, Ellen," Daisy said at once. "I did forget myself."

"You see, we're not the only ones who think he's a bastard," Aaron whispered to Brenda, who whispered back, "Stay out of this, Aaron."

Cynthia clasped and unclasped her hands. Unbearable hostility surrounded her. Even her grandfather, looking out of his gold frame, seemed suddenly to be cold and angry, which was, she knew, absurd, for he had been a kindly man who worked in his fancy little garden and gave her his prize strawberries, warm from the sun, for breakfast.

She had to get out of this room. "I'm going for a little walk," she said.

Daisy cried, "No, Cindy, no! The minute your father comes out, we're leaving. I don't want to have to go looking for you."

"I'll only go as far as the pond. You can see me from this window. Excuse me, everyone, please."

On their broad black feet two swans slid over the ice as if they were on skates. The remains of cut-up bread lay on the grass at the pond's edge. Gran fed them all winter when, because the pond was frozen, they were unable to reach underwater to feed themselves. Cynthia watched them until they reached a circle of water where those few of their young who had not yet been sent away to fend for themselves were floating. The tranquillity of these creatures and the peace of the wintry silence relieved her tension. A strong wind blew, but there was no rustle of leafage. There were no birdcalls. And she stood still, hearing the silence.

Sometimes she thought of going away to a place where she knew no one and no one knew her. She imagined a cold place, in Alaska perhaps, near a glacial lake where eagles nested in the trees. She thought of a warm place on an untouristed island, where the surf rolled and broke on a quiet beach. Like a primitive person you would just live there, simply live out each day; and all the days would roll on with little memory of the past or need to care about what was to happen in the future.

Naturally she knew, even as she was having these escapist daydreams, that they were foolish. She knew as well as anyone could that the best, maybe the only, way to be rid of such malaise is to work and be involved with other people. But she had been doing just that, she had not been thinking only of herself or feeling sorry for herself; self-pity was disgusting.

Yet she had not been healed. . . .

The wind was rising. It was terribly cold, so that she drew her coat tightly about her. It was a fine, warm coat of gray cashmere, so enormously expensive that she had hesitated to buy it. But when you worked in the fashion world, you could not avoid some extravagances; they were part of the job. All of that was long ago in another life, to which she never wanted to return.

And she started back toward the house, thinking that something must have been resolved in there by now, most probably for the worst. She felt so sorry for Gran, naive, hopeful Gran, who was trying so hard to arrange everything for the best.

Another car, a black Jaguar, had been added to the three in the driveway. At the sight of it she stopped short. It could not possibly be Andrew's car. . . . But of course, it was. She went weak with outrage. Impulsively, she went toward the kitchen door with the intention of hiding, but that made no sense because they would be looking all over for her in order to start home. And straightening her shoulders, she marched boldly through the front door into the hall.

Andrew was standing there with Jenny. Evidently he had just arrived because he was still wearing his fleece jacket. She had a flash of recall: a windy Saturday, a search for a double stroller, and after they had bought it, the purchase of the red fleece jacket. Now she had a quick flash of his startled face, flushed by the wind, with dark circles under his eyes.

Furiously, she demanded, "What do you think you are doing here?"

"I don't know. I was invited to come. Your grandmother telephoned. I had no idea what she wanted. She didn't say."

"Fine story. You didn't know I'd be here?"

"No, I didn't." He gave her a tentative smile. He was being conciliatory, as if he were not sure what she was going to do. And she could have struck the smile off his face.

"I don't believe you," she said. "You and my grandmother, who seems to have lost her mind, cooked this up between you."

"I can't help it if you don't believe it, but it's the truth. I'm staying for the weekend at Jack Owens's house, and your grandmother happened to meet Mary Owens in the village. That's how she knew I was with them, and she phoned me."

"Well, now that you've come, you should turn right around and go."

"I can't very well do that until I've seen your grandmother, can I, now, Cindy?"

"I am not Cindy to you, I am Cynthia. Or better still, I am nobody at all."

"Cynthia—can't we please talk quietly and sensibly?"

"No. No. Was there anything 'sensible' in what you did that night? I was down, as I thought you were, too, all the way down in a dark hole after we lost our children—and I was just beginning to climb up and see a trace of light, just beginning—"

"You were? But you never told me. I never saw—"

"I never got the chance that night when you thrust me back down with my face in the mud. In mud! You did that to me. And you—now you come using words like *sensible*."

"Cynthia!" Daisy's voice rang from the guest closet at the back of the hall. "We're just getting our coats—why, what on earth are you doing here?" she cried, seeing Andrew.

Lewis strode down the hall, his voice booming. "What the devil are you doing here? Haven't you done enough to my daughter without following her?"

Now Annette came running with her glasses

sliding down her nose. "Stop, Lewis! He's not doing anything to Cynthia. I invited him."

"You what? Now I've heard everything. You
have done more harmful mischief this morning,
Mother. I'm speechless."

Suddenly the hall, which was long and almost
as wide as an average room, was as crowded as a
highway at rush hour; there could not have been
more than a dozen people in it, but they all, even
Ellen with Freddie in her arms, came jostling out
of various doors toward the little group at the
front, toward the loud anger.

"Oh, Gran," cried Cynthia, "oh, Gran, what
have you done to me? Why did you do this? You
knew all about—"

"Yes, I knew. That's why I did it."

Mortified by this public display of her most
private emotions, Cynthia began to cry.

Daisy put her arms about her daughter. "This
whole morning has been a circus. Disgusting.
We're leaving. This is it. Your presence, Andrew,"
she said icily, "is the last straw." And she turned
toward Annette. "We have to take Cynthia home.
Right now. And, Andrew, you stay away from

her. You came here snooping, for what I don't know, but stay away from her. I mean it."

"That's between Cynthia and me, Mom."

"What right have you to call her 'Mom'?" demanded Lewis. "You forfeited that right when you behaved like an animal that night—"

"Please, please," Annette pleaded. "All right, I made a bad mistake. I meant well." Her eyes filled, and she took a white lace handkerchief out of her cuff to wipe them.

"I'll go," Andrew said. "This is too much for you. For everybody."

But Annette seized his lapel. "No, I asked you to come, and I don't want you to go like this. You haven't done anything wrong. No."

Aaron was feeling pity. It was a shame to see an old person attacked. He saw that sometimes in his practice, and he was never able to keep his mouth shut.

" 'Be not hasty in thy spirit to be angry,' " he said now, loud enough for everyone to hear.

Lewis snapped. "Most of us are well acquainted with the Bible, thank you very much."

"This is a crazy house." This time Aaron whispered. "I told you, Brenda, I didn't want to come here."

Brenda sighed ruefully. "Ah people, people. It's tragic, that's all it is."

"Disgraceful. Yelling like savages."

"Don't you think you ever did some ranting and yelling?"

"Well, maybe, but not like this."

"Honey, you were so loud when Mark ran off and married Ellen that I was afraid the neighbors would hear. The people across the hall, if you want to know, did hear."

Annette wiped her flowing eyes. As tall and erect as she was, she seemed suddenly very small.

"Papa Gene," Lucy cried, for Gene had come out of another door under the stairs. "Gran is crying."

"Good God, Brenda, here's my best friend," Aaron muttered as he and Gene caught sight of each other.

"Do hush," said Brenda. "We're stuck here till tomorrow."

"Why can't we leave now?"

"Drive all that way back with Freddie? The

trip up was too long as it is. And besides, they're predicting a storm."

Gene called over somebody's head, "Did you know about this assemblage, Mark?"

"Only that we were invited. We and my parents."

"Interesting," Gene muttered. "Very interesting." And then, turning to Annette, he put his arm around her. "Don't cry, Mother. Everybody knows you meant well. It just hasn't worked, but that's no fault of yours. I think it's best now that we all go home and let your house be peaceful again. Go take a rest and don't make yourself sick over a failed experiment. It's not worth it. I told you, I'm coming next week to spend the day with you. I promise."

You don't have to keep your promise as far as I'm concerned, she thought, but did not say, being at the stage in which a sorrowful, defeated person throws up his hands and cries: *I don't care. Now let everything go to smash. It doesn't matter to me anymore.* She had tried tough love with her sons, but it had not worked. She had hoped that within Andrew and Cynthia, as they saw each other, a bit of their original fire would spark again. Nothing had worked, they were all going away, and let that be the end of it.

At that moment Marian came almost flying out of the dining room.

"What's this?" she cried. "People are leaving? Why, lunch is already on the table."

In spite of her tears Annette recovered her dignity as a hostess. In a most gracious tone she said, "Some of you know my dear friend Marian Lester."

"I do! I do! You gave me that doll with the straw hat on. I was going to bring it, but Mama said it was too big to fit in the bag and wouldn't let me." Lucy chattered on. "I'm getting a boy doll just as big for my birthday. Papa Gene's giving it to me, aren't you, Papa Gene? Why are you putting your coat on? Aren't you going to stay for lunch? Grandpa and Grandma are staying. We're going to be here until tomorrow morning. Aren't you?"

"Well," Gene began, thinking, What a fine pickle, damn it, when Marian mounted the first step and clapped her hands.

"You people can't walk out like this. You simply can't do this to Annette," she said like the schoolteacher she was. "Jenny has made a beautiful lunch, to which you were all invited. You all accepted the invitation, so do, please, put your coats away."

Well, well, thought Daisy, and just who does she think she is, to order us around as if we were in her kindergarten?

Gene chuckled to himself. Hasn't she got nerve, though? I seem to remember she's a teacher. Claps her hands like one. But pretty. That tilted, pert little nose . . .

"Mrs. Lester," said Lewis, "I do understand, but my daughter isn't feeling well, and we really need to get her home."

Marian was not to be deterred. "It's after twelve, and you've a long ride back to the city. You'd certainly need to stop off on the way for something to eat. So you'd do a lot better to have a nice lunch now before you leave."

"Yes, do," urged Ellen, who was hoping that maybe Cynthia and Andrew would make some move, although it certainly didn't look now as though they ever could.

"You can't do this to Annette, or to Jenny, either, after all her work." Marian spoke sternly.

"You simply can't. If some of you can't stand one another—you see, I know all about many things —you can go separately into the dining room. It's a buffet lunch. Take what you want and go wherever you want to eat it. Some of you are talking to each other and you can get together. There are enough rooms in this house so you can all spread out."

"I guess we'll have to stay, Mother," said Cynthia, who was pained by the sight of Gran's woebegone face.

"I don't see how you can forgive her for this trick," replied Daisy, tossing her head in Andrew's direction.

"I don't forgive her, exactly, but I feel terribly sorry for her."

"Then you're more tolerant than I am. If she were not so old, I would give her a piece of my mind. Does she think it amusing to do this sort of thing?"

Lewis upbraided his wife. "Don't be absurd. You know her better than that. Now, come on," he said irritably, and, propelling his wife and daughter ahead of him, marched them into the dining room.

A few minutes later he marched them out again. Holding their plates, the three retired to eat by themselves in Annette's snuggery.

In the dining room the long table was set with bowls and platters bearing sliced cold meats, a hot chicken pie, a huge, crisp vegetable salad, warm breads of three different kinds, molasses cookies, peach cake, and a mélange of fresh fruit. The bowls and platters were old porcelain, Annette's best. At the heart of their arrangement was an overflowing cluster of cream-colored roses.

"Done herself proud, as they say," remarked Andrew to himself. There had been some slight confusion in the hall as to who would go to the table after the first three and how some of them would avoid each other. Shaken by seeing his wife again—Andrew still thought of Cynthia as "my wife," not only because under the law she still was, but also because he still felt attached to her—Andrew stood at the foot of the stairs with his plate, uncertain of where he was expected to go. He was pulled about by ill-assorted emotions, sadness, a certain amount of anger, and a miserable embarrassment over feeling superfluous. If he could decently have fled from the house, he would have done so.

Just then Gene had given him a warm greeting. "Andrew! Haven't seen you for too long," he cried, thinking at the same time that it was a pity that Lewis wasn't near enough to see the warmth of the greeting. "Come join us. Ellen and Mark are going to eat in the sunroom. Stone floor, you see, so in case Lucy spills, as she usually does, it won't do any damage. Come on, let's hurry."

Even in his present frame of mind Andrew had been able to feel amusement at the "hurry," which clearly meant, "Hurry before Mark's parents get there first and shut me out."

Those parents of Mark's were the last to go to the table.

"Heaven only knows what they'll have to eat," Aaron grumbled. "Shrimp salad, most likely."

"Well, you're fat enough to go without one lunch if you have to," Brenda told him. At this point she had begun to feel the prevailing nasty mood.

But to Aaron's great relief, since he had had a

very early breakfast, he found plenty of salad and fruit that he could eat.

These they took to the library, which, because they had already spent time there, seemed a little familiar. Nevertheless, they were feeling rather forlorn, when Mark came in with Lucy. He sat down and took a mouthful of food before he looked up over the plate and smiled at them. The smile, as both of them knew very well, was his way of telling them that he understood their discomfort. They were thinking how different it would be if he had married Jennifer Cohen. Well, it would be different for Ellen, too, if she had married that other guy. She would probably be living in Paris, on the Place de Something-or-Other.

After a minute he said, "We're all feeling dreary. It's a very strange situation, to say the least."

"There seems to be more than one strange situation," Aaron responded.

"Weird," Brenda said. "That young couple. You would think that after their tragedy, they would cling to each other."

Aaron objected. "It's not that simple. You're a

social worker, and you don't know about complex relationships?"

"Well, of course I do. Something else must have happened afterward. Of course."

"It did, but not now." And Mark looked significantly toward Lucy.

Brenda shuddered. "It feels as if somebody has just died in this house."

"Don't worry," Mark said. "They'll all be rushing home in a few minutes. They want to beat the weather."

The room was growing noticeably darker, and he got up to turn on the lights. Outside, the sky was iron-gray, hard and somber. Conversation seemed to wilt as the little group, with their plates on their laps, contemplated that sky. Even Lucy, thoughtfully chewing molasses cookies, was drawn into the silence.

They all looked up when Annette came in. She was traveling from one room to the other, trying to act as though it were perfectly natural for people to be thus dispersed. Having powdered her nose and removed all signs of tears, she had resolved to see things through with dignity to the end. Admittedly, she had been saved by Marian, who now, in the dining room, was presiding over the tea- and coffeepots.

"How are you all doing?" she asked cheerfully. "Is everyone having enough to eat?"

Lucy jumped up. "I'm not. I need some cake."

"Well, of course you do. Come on with me, and I'll get some for you."

"Grandpa, you come too. We'll get some for Papa Gene. He likes cake."

For a moment no one answered, and then Mark said quickly, "Grandpa's still eating. You and Gran go do it."

Now Lucy directed her frown toward Aaron. "You never want to go see Papa Gene. You never do."

At that Annette took her hand. "Come on," she said firmly. "The cake will be all gone if we don't hurry."

"We forget what children observe," Brenda remarked when they left. "Without actually understanding, they can detect so much that we think we're hiding. It's even said that infants can sense moods from indifferent handling or angry voices. . . ." Her own voice dwindled away. Neither her husband nor her son refuted her.

Not at our house, Mark was thinking. Our children are safe from all that. His plump baby boy and his spirited, small Lucy were safe.

"Let him go, dear," Ellen said, for Lucy, kissing Freddie, was smearing the remains of a chocolate bonbon on his cheek.

It was really remarkable, considering all you heard and read about sibling jealousy, that Lucy had accepted Freddie's arrival so well. Spunky and rough as she could be when playing with her friends, with him she was gentle and affectionate. Perhaps, Ellen thought, it is because she sees and receives so much affection at home.

"I'm bored," Lucy said.

Gene chuckled. "Now, where did she ever get that?"

"I can't imagine. She certainly hasn't heard it from me. I never have time enough to get bored."

"What's this?" Annette, still on her room-to-room tour, had just come in. "Bored? Well, naturally she is. Now that she's had lunch, there's nothing for her to do. Why don't you take her to see the swans, Ellen?"

"It's freezing outside," said Gene, protective as usual.

"Nonsense. As long as she's warmly dressed, a little fresh, cold air will be good for her. It'll be good for Freddie too."

Ellen, agreeing and glad to get out of the house, went for the clothes. She had been feeling too uneasy for comfort, uneasy and even apprehensive, as if something were going to *happen*. It was not usual for her to exaggerate worries, but today was exceptional. As long as so many enemies were under one roof, there could be an explosion.

Here sat Andrew, watching Freddie with a wistful smile on his serious face, and God only knew what anguish within; Andrew, the cause of Cynthia's disillusionment and the object of her parents' wrath.

An overheard remark might ignite either Lewis or Ellen's own father, who in turn might do or say something that would inflame Lewis or Aaron; or Aaron might in some way offend her father.

There was no end to it. With all that pain and

anger, even people who thought themselves civilized were capable of doing crazy things. . . .

Outdoors she took a long breath of cold air. The brown, frozen grass crackled under her feet as, walking carefully, she carried Freddie downhill toward the pond. Lucy, as usual, ran far ahead.

Even in December it was beautiful here. When trees were bare, one saw the true grace of their branches, upraised like arms. Crows, surely not pretty birds, had their own grace, too, as they rose from their perches and sped down the sky. In the woods that framed Gran's property there was, to an eye aware of colors, among the pines and spruce, the hemlock and firs, an abundance of greens: olive and grass and moss; there was even the dusty blue of a single Colorado spruce, an exotic loner among all those native greens. It could not have grown there by natural accident; her grandfather must have planted it. I should paint that sometime, she thought, exactly as it is, or maybe, better still, in the flicker of summer sun and shade.

All those people cooped up in the house right now could be taking a hike through the woods on the trail that Gran kept cleared for the Scouts. But no, they were nursing their grievances instead, some of them so old that they would never be uprooted. It would be easier to uproot that spruce with a toy shovel.

Near the edge of the pond there was a rock, remembered from Ellen's childhood, with a flat ledge on which one could sit. From there you could see the whole pond as far as the juncture with the larger lake.

"Sit down for a minute with me," she said to Lucy, "and look around. Tell me what you see."

After making a full circle turn Lucy said, "You told me the leaves all fall off when it's cold, but that tree has leaves."

"It's called a pin oak, and it's the only one that loses its leaves in the spring, when all the other trees are getting new ones."

"Why?"

"I really don't know. I'll find out, though, and then I'll tell you."

And she would have to find out, because Lucy would be sure to remember and ask her. She was an intense little girl, eager and curious. They had not needed the school psychologist to tell them how very bright she was. Ellen smiled to herself, thinking that it required a deal of energy to keep up with this first-grader. Freddie, on the other hand, was quite different; a much more placid baby than Lucy had ever been, he was sitting comfortably on her lap with the pacifier in his mouth.

"It's too cold," Lucy said.

"You're right. It's growing colder. Let's walk around the edge, nearer to the swans, and then hurry back to the house."

It was so quiet and calm here alone with her children! She was reluctant to leave it. But a fine sleet was now starting to fall, stinging one's face.

"Come on, let's run. See? The swans made a long path, breaking the ice, so they can swim. They do it pushing with their chests. It's hard work."

Three floated, their orange beaks proud and high, their ruffle-edged white wings like ballet skirts.

"Those must be the father and mother with one of their grown children who hasn't flown away yet," Ellen explained. "Aren't they beautiful?"

"I want to pet one."

"Oh, you can't. They're swimming."

"But if they walk over here on the ice?"

"You mustn't. They don't like it. Swans can be fierce. Even the dogs are afraid of them."

"Do they bark at the dogs?"

"No, these are mute swans. That means they don't make much noise, just grunts sometimes. When they're babies, they peep a little, that's all."

"Where do the babies live?"

"In a nest, the same as little birds do. You remember the nest they showed you at school."

"A swan's nest has to be much bigger," Lucy observed.

"Much bigger. About as big as our sofa at home."

"Where is it?"

"Way over on the other side. I don't think it's even there anymore in the winter."

"Let's look for it."

"Not now. Hey, the sleet's really coming down. Let's run."

"I want to see the nest."

"No, Lucy. I said no."

"But I'll be right back, I promise."

"No, Lucy!"

"Right back, Mommy!" And she was gone, racing over the ice toward the swans.

"Come back! Back, Lucy!" screamed Ellen.

In horror, screaming, tearing her throat, she stood there as Lucy ran; the swans, with a great splash and spread of wings, rose into the air when Lucy plunged and disappeared. Black water closed over her. . . . For an instant Ellen looked wildly about. Then, setting the heavy baby down on the grass, she ran onto the ice, slipped, fell, got up, and slid into the water.

In the library Mark and his parents were still a group apart. He was on the window seat looking out toward the pond, musing to himself.

"What a queer situation I'm in today. I've always liked Cynthia, and I like Andy too. We used to play tennis sometimes, singles on Sunday mornings. But I can't very well go talk to either of them without hurting the other."

Brenda sighed. "Poor souls. To lose a child— that's the worst of all."

Half hearing, Aaron shuddered. "Two of them."

He had been absorbed in his own thoughts, feeling the atmosphere of this house, this room with its portraits and books. He was thinking about the people who had lived here, old-line Americans, at home for generations in the same neighborhood among trees that were centuries old. It must be a good feeling, he thought without envy, merely ruminating. In a locked glass-fronted bookcase apart from the rest of the books in the room, he read titles: Dickens, Balzac, Thackeray. . . . How is it that a man brought up with all these good things can be as hateful as Gene Byrne?

Then at once came the retort: And what made you so hateful toward him, Aaron? You were never brought up to hate.

"Look," he said, beckoning to his son. "These must be first editions, don't you think? What a treasure! All these great minds—"

It was exactly then, in the middle of a sentence, that he heard his son's dreadful cry.

"What— What?"

"In the pond. Oh, God, they've fallen in!"

Brenda screamed and ran to the window. "Where? Where? I don't see—"

But Mark and Aaron were already fleeing through the hall and out, down the steps to the lawn.

In the hall, doors were opening. From the kitchen, the snuggery, the sunroom, and from everywhere, people were staring.

"What is it? What happened?"

"What on earth?" Gene cried. Brenda's screams had annoyed him. "What's all this racket?"

"Ellen!" Brenda screamed back at him. "Ellen —they've fallen into the pond!"

Then everyone ran. Without coats they ran out into the falling sleet, stumbling and sliding down the hill behind Mark and Aaron.

The channel of water was narrow, not much wider than the swan who had forced it open. One edge was jagged, where the ice had broken under Ellen's weight as she plunged in. Now Mark plunged in to grasp Ellen as, in her thick down jacket and heavy shoes, she struggled.

"Lucy! Lucy!" she implored.

"Rope! Rope!" Lewis cried helplessly.

Under his weight a piece of ice had cracked,

and he jumped backward. On either side of the channel the ice was crumbling.

Andrew came running with rope. "In my trunk." He gasped. "Can you reach—" And he held the rope out to Mark.

"No! No! It's Lucy." He was weeping. "She wouldn't—"

At once Andrew grasped his meaning. *She wouldn't know enough to catch or hold on to the rope.* The pond was fifteen or twenty feet deep. The child was at the bottom. What if the rope were not long enough anyway?

The four men, for Gene had come up behind the others, stood for a second as if mesmerized by despair until Andrew, prepared to jump in, took off his shoes and was then abruptly pushed aside.

"Let me. Tie the rope around my waist," Daisy commanded. She dropped her shoes and her skirt. "Pray God it's long enough. Tie it as low as you can. Give me three minutes. If I haven't jerked the rope, pull me up."

Ellen had collapsed onto Mark's shoulder. Aaron and Gene were trying to pull them both up onto the ice, but without a rope it was almost impossible. Meanwhile, Andrew was holding with both hands on to the rope, which had by now grown taut. The rope was either too short, or else Daisy had reached the bottom and perhaps—only perhaps—found Lucy.

There was no sound except for the steady tinkling of sleet upon the ice. The horrified little group of watchers on the rapidly whitening grass stood speechless and unmoving in the arctic cold. Like people watching a disabled plane attempt a landing while emergency equipment was prepared for disaster, their eyes were large and their lips hung open. Even the dogs stood still, as if they knew that something out of the ordinary was happening.

After who knew how long, Andrew felt a tug on the rope. "She's pulling!" he shouted. And when Lewis sprang to help him, protested, "No, let me. I'm younger than you, and you've got a bad back."

Instantly, Gene sprang to help, leaving Mark with one arm around Ellen and the other forearm resting in a vain attempt to lift himself onto the slippery ice. Together, gradually, Andrew and the two brothers pulled, fought for footing, slipped, fell, got up and pulled some more, until at last

Daisy's head appeared above the water. She was blue in the face. Her hair streamed and she had no breath left, but she was holding Lucy to her chest.

From the huddled group of women on the grass came a cry. All, even Jenny, came running. Gene seized Lucy, while Daisy, her chest heaving, sank down on the ice.

"Get back, all of you," warned Andrew. "It's not solid so near the edge. Get back."

The little girl lay lifeless, her long hair dripping and her legs dangling in Gene's arms. "Oh, God," he groaned, "she isn't breathing."

Aaron snatched her away from Gene. "Give her to me." And he began to run toward the grass.

"If someone, for Christ's sake," Mark yelled, "will take Ellen, please? I can't hold on much longer."

Andrew and Lewis, who had been tending Daisy, ran with the rope, tied it tightly around the two of them and pulled. Mark, faint from exhaustion and cold, stumbled onto the ice. Ellen was unconscious.

"My God," Andrew murmured, "the water's got to be thirty-two degrees."

All was helter-skelter. Then Aaron, tense and brusque, laid Lucy on the grass and took command.

"Lay Ellen down. Somebody get Daisy back to the house. Quick! She needs warm, dry clothes, blankets, and hot drinks. Right now!" The words came out like bullets. "You—what's your name—Andrew, can you do mouth-to-mouth resuscitation?"

"No, but if you show me, I can—"

Lewis broke in. "I've done it. Where shall I—"

"Then let Andrew take your wife to the house. You, Lewis, do Ellen. I'll take the baby. Hurry, hurry, hurry!" Neither mother nor child, lying side by side, was breathing. "Do what I do. Look. Move the head back and forth as far as you can. Watch me. Back and forth. Back and forth. Open the airway. Pinch the nose. No, like this. Pinch. Now fit your mouth on hers, tight fit, blow. Get the air flow. . . ."

Sleet poured over Aaron, who knelt there trying to pour life into his little grandchild, and over

Lewis, who was doing the same for his brother's child.

Gene and the women stood waiting, trembling in their light clothing. No one stirred. Annette wept silently. Mark was supine on the grass. Cynthia, clutching the baby, watched her father. In awe Brenda watched her husband; she was confident; if it could be done, Aaron would do it.

Time passed; whether it measured two minutes or twenty, no one there would ever be able to estimate. They would say only that it was an eternity.

Suddenly, Lucy struggled and coughed. A stream of water flew out of her lungs; she began to cry, and vomited. Mark forced himself to his tottering legs and took her, wet, sobbing, and shaking, into his arms.

A few minutes later Ellen brought up a stream of water. In confusion she tried to rise, and then, as she opened her eyes and reality flowed back, she became hysterical.

"Lucy! Where's Lucy? Where's Freddie? Oh, for God's sake, what happened to Freddie, I left him—"

"Freddie's fine. Cynthia has him. And Lucy's

right here. Look. She's all right too. Take it easy, Ellen. Take it easy," Lewis whispered. "There she is with Mark. And here's your father."

"We need a car, we need help," Aaron said. "They can't walk back."

But Marian, practical Marian, had thought of that and was already partway up the hill toward the parked cars. A few moments later her four-wheel drive came bumping over the grass, and Ellen, with Lucy clinging to her, was lifted in.

"The rest of us had better hotfoot it to the house," Aaron said. "We've been out here for a good twenty minutes or more, and hypothermia is no joke."

Soaked and shivering, with frozen fingers and feet, all those who could not fit into the Jeep ran toward the house.

An hour later everyone was gathered in the library, where Jenny, while the survivors were being cared for upstairs, had built a grand log fire. Close to its heat and crackle a big chair held Ellen with Lucy on her lap, both of them drowsing under a thick red blanket. On the other side of the fireplace, in a pair of similar chairs and also covered with blankets, sat Mark and Daisy, with Freddie and a pile of blocks on the floor between them. On a table within easy reach was a large tray with a varied assortment of hot drinks, ranging from brandy to coffee to cocoa for Lucy. Annette, remembering that sugar was the quick remedy for exhaustion, had added a plate of sugar cookies.

"What else can a person like me, at my age, do but give food?" she asked Marian. "I should be doing something more, but I don't know what. I'm still trembling, and I feel useless."

"Useless? You're the last person to say that about herself."

"My loyal friend is speaking."

"No, it's the truth."

"I couldn't have managed today without your help, Marian."

"It wasn't much, but I'm glad I could do it. Now I'd better go home."

"You're sure you won't stay to dinner?"

"I'll stay another half hour. But the weather's getting worse, and I want to get back before dark."

The room was very still except for the sound of

the fire. Those near to it were recuperating, and the others, Annette thought, were naturally respecting their rest. But it also occurred to her that this was the first time since any of them had entered the house today when they had all been in one room together. They were still scattered over a large space. Gene was on the sofa next to her. Andrew had drawn a straight chair near to the sofa, with the dogs at his feet. Cynthia, as far away from Andrew as she could get, was with her father on the other side of the room, near Daisy; they made a loose grouping with Aaron and Brenda. Such remarks as were made among them all were murmured and inaudible at Annette's end of the room. After the day's shock, she supposed, when during those awful minutes at the scene we all stood in total silence wondering whether Ellen and Lucy were alive, this would be a normal reaction; or would it be more normal now to let one's emotions bubble and bubble over? She really did not know. She only knew that somebody must eventually say something.

So she raised her voice loud enough to be heard by everyone and inquired, "Are you all feeling any warmer?"

Aaron Sachs responded, "I know I am, but how are you, Mrs. Byrne?"

"Daisy," said Daisy in her crisp fashion. "And I'm fine, thank you."

"You're my all-time heroine, Aunt Daisy," Mark told her. "For the rest of my life . . . I don't know . . . I can't express it."

"Two and three quarter minutes by my watch without taking a breath," Andrew said. "Right up to the limit."

"A heroine," Aaron echoed. "A heroine with good lungs."

Annette glanced at Gene, who cleared his throat and leaned down to stroke Roscoe's head. When he looked up, he spoke almost shyly. "Yes. It seems that there are no better words than *thank you*, Daisy. Two syllables to weigh against a child's life." His voice broke. "Thank you. Thank you, Daisy."

For another few minutes no one spoke. Then Lewis was heard.

"There were a couple of young fellows at the club who went in for swimming under ice. Kind of crazy—very crazy. But Daisy did it one day.

They showed her how. I was angry at her. She'll dare anything, Daisy will."

A little prickle of shame went down Annette's back. What right had she had in the first place to sniff, even mentally, at Daisy's "boarding school and country club" athletics? Just because she isn't like me, she scolded, I felt myself superior, a more "serious" person. My God, if we all would just take a good, honest look at ourselves, we might not always like what we see.

"Hypothermia can put you in the hospital in a few minutes," Aaron was saying. "That's all you need."

Andrew mused, "Funny. When I cleaned the trunk of my car, I was going to take the rope out. I had it there from the time I got stuck in a snowbank. It was on a ski trip in Vermont," he added irrelevantly, and added again, "Lucky thing I didn't."

"I never learned to swim underwater," said Mark. "Never learned to resuscitate either. Now I mean to do it."

"Red Cross," Lewis advised. "Daisy and I took a course. Very enjoyable too."

They were all speaking without looking at one

another. It was as if, Annette thought, they were addressing a public gathering, or perhaps simply talking to the air, or maybe just thinking out loud.

Cynthia was silent. She was watching Freddie, who, after many patient trials, had managed to build a tower of three blocks. And she tried to remember what she had read in one of her many books—long since given away—about the various stages of child development. What foolish worries we have! As if it matters whether a beautiful, healthy baby like this one is a bit smarter or a bit slower than the baby next door. His cheeks that had been red from the cold were now red from the heat. With a happy laugh he knocked the tower down. Then he began to build it again. She could not take her eyes away from him.

Yet she was aware that Andrew had craned his head in her direction. Whether he was looking at her or at Freddie, she was unable to tell, but it made no difference either way. He didn't belong here.

I should see more of Ellen and Mark, she thought. Somehow, God only knows how, this sight of Freddie, my picking him up when he was crying there on the grass, has changed me. I never thought I could bear to hold a baby again.

"It's time for his supper," Mark said, standing up.

Cynthia said quickly, "If you'll tell me what he eats, I'll give it to him."

Mark smiled. "You want to, don't you?"

"Yes. May I?"

She saw, when he nodded, that he understood her. "He gets junior food, and after that a bottle. Everything's in our tote bag in the hall. Wait. I'll give it to you."

"No, I'll find it. He'll go with me. He likes me."

"Jenny has the high chair," Annette called.

On Cynthia's lap in the snuggery Freddie was already having his bottle when Marian, in coat and boots, passed the door.

"Pretty sight," she called.

"Come in for a second. I want to thank you for helping Gran today. And for all the rest too."

"Wasn't it a horrendous day? And yet, crazy as it sounds, maybe some good will have come out of it."

"I have a feeling it will. Uncle Gene and my

father have got to do a lot of thinking after this. In fact, it seemed to me in there that they already have begun."

"Death, or even the prospect of it, has a mighty powerful effect on people. I never realized how powerful until it hit me."

"I think Gran said you're a widow?"

"A sudden widow. We went to the city for a weekend vacation, had a wonderful dinner, saw a wonderful play, and went happily to bed in our hotel room. Toward morning I heard him get up, walk across the room, and fall."

Marian sat down on the edge of a chair. Her face was without expression, and strangely, that seemed to move Cynthia more than tears might have done.

"He was tall, thin, and blond, part Scandinavian, and athletic. One of those people who you think are made to live long."

"How awful for you."

"Sometimes I was angry at him. So many hours, so many days wasted . . . And now gone. Forever. Never." She threw out her hands, palms up. "And that's it." Then she rose, and, suddenly brisk and businesslike in her customary way, she concluded, "I don't know why I got started on this. I'm sorry. That's a sweet boy. Lovely eyes. I'd better run. It's already dark."

Why I got started. Cynthia smiled wryly. You wanted to teach me a lesson, that's why. But it won't work, Marian. No, because my situation is entirely different. Entirely.

When she carried Freddie back into the library, Ellen, awake now, took him from her, leaving her with empty hands. A bad feeling of utter detachment swept over her. And she stood uncertainly, hearing the fierce wind shake the windowpanes.

"I wouldn't want to be out in a car tonight," Annette remarked.

Andrew said promptly, "That reminds me. I'd better say good-bye to you all and start right now."

"Absolutely not," Annette protested, thinking: He wants to leave because Cynthia won't even look at him. "That's a ten-mile drive, and Jenny just heard on the radio that the roads are all ice. There's plenty of room for you. This house is elastic. It stretches to fit." And as he hesitated, she added with deliberate tactlessness, "You know that. You've been here often enough. Just sit down, Andrew."

There came a restless stir in the room, as if everyone had sat too long or, having said all they were capable of saying, were uncomfortably aware of what was still unsaid.

Brenda was folding the red blankets that were no longer in use. And Annette made an announcement.

"Brenda has been making up beds for all you people tonight. Can you imagine? When I went upstairs, I found her working. You shouldn't have, Brenda."

"Well, Jenny is busy enough in the kitchen, and this really is a mob. Don't worry, your linen closet is still neat. I am the original fusspot—Aaron, don't sit in that chair, what are you thinking of? Your suit is still wet."

Aaron bounced up. "I know it, but what am I going to do? I didn't bring another suit."

"Oh, my, you're soaked," cried Annette. "Doesn't anyone, can't anyone—" And she looked around the room in appeal. "You're the nearest to his size, Gene."

Embarrassed, Aaron laughed. "Only a six-inch difference."

Gene, fidgeting, fussed over Roscoe, which was something that, not being a dog person, he did not usually do. "I keep a few things here. I'll find something," he said, looking self-conscious.

"So that's solved," said Annette.

We'll see what happens at dinner, she thought. I'm not sure of anything, but we have made some progress, at least. . . .

"Why don't we go up and rest?" she said cheerfully. "If you want to, I mean. I think we all deserve a rest. As for me, I need a nap before dinner. It's at seven."

The lunch table had been transformed for dinner, thought Andrew, who noticed such things, much as a woman wearing a sweater and skirt, however becoming, is transformed by a ballgown. Candles in silver holders glowed on pale yellow china edged in the Greek key pattern. The cream-colored roses in the large bowl had been augmented by smaller clusters going down the center of the table. Once again Annette had "done herself proud." She might as well, he thought somewhat bitterly, have been adorning a wedding reception. . . . As indeed, she had once done.

With her customary attention to household details Annette surveyed the table and was satisfied. Very infrequently these days were festive meals served in this lovely room that had for so many years been used to bright lights and bright conversation. Life was quiet now in this house where she lived with Jenny and the dogs. And she thought again, Okay, there's been progress since our near disaster today. But let's see what happens next.

"We'll serve ourselves from the sideboard and then sit wherever we want," she said. "Gene, will you do the wine? And, Lewis, you're a good carver, so please do the roast."

"Ah, roast beef," sighed Lewis. "The cholesterol special. But I love it. The first I've had in six months."

"Aaron and Brenda, there's pasta for you. Jenny makes a marvelous red sauce without meat. And we've lots of vegetables," Annette assured them. At the same time she could scarcely keep from laughing because Aaron looked so ridiculous in the borrowed suit.

"If you want to laugh, go ahead," Aaron said. "I had a glimpse of myself in the mirror on the way downstairs."

"Are you some sort of mind-reader? Well, to tell the truth—"

Now Aaron laughed. "You don't have to say so, everyone can see it."

The trousers, at least six inches too long, were fastened up with safety pins. At the waist another large blanket pin, borrowed from Freddie's tote bag, kept the trousers from falling down.

"Of course, as long as I sit no one can see it, so that saves my dignity."

"Tell me, how is the pasta?"

"Perfect, thank you."

"You went to so much trouble for us," Brenda said.

"It was no trouble at all. It was a pleasure."

Mark, observing from the other end of the table, had a sudden surge of pride in his mother. She was a gracious woman. He had never given any thought to her public persona, to how she might look to other people—not counting his father-in-law, and well he knew what that man's prejudice had been! There she sat, quiet and confident in her fine dark dress and her narrow necklace of sculptured gold. And he felt a great tenderness for her.

Tenderness overflowed in him. Here were Ellen, his darling, and Lucy sitting high on Annette's two-volume *Oxford English Dictionary,* and Freddie safely asleep upstairs in the portable crib; it went without saying that these had always been far more precious to him than was his own life. Tonight, though, it seemed as if his capacity to feel a unity with other human beings had expanded, too, so that, in varying degrees, he felt able to say that he "loved"—however you wanted to define *love*—every soul in the room.

Annette, reading his expression, was moved by it. And again she thought she felt a kind of loosening in the atmosphere: people—twelve of them, a nice tidy number around the table—were beginning to converse a bit. She became suddenly aware that she had been sitting with strained, tight muscles, and must relax.

They all looked so *civilized.* And these were the same people, the same group, that had been so *savage* in the front hall this morning. Maybe they had been having some serious reflections during that little nap time. . . .

Her eyes roved from her two sons—was it purely an accident that had brought them to be sitting next to each other?—to Lucy in her pink dress, to the bronze lights in Ellen's hair, to Aaron Sachs's neat beard, and her eyes were satisfied.

When they reached Cynthia—ah, that was another matter! Perfect in gray silk and appropriate pearls, she sat like a statue, cool, remote, and without expression. And in Annette's heart there was a painful contest between compassion and impatience. Cynthia's father and mother, apparently, had taken steps toward Andrew. And yet, who was a mere grandmother to judge?

"Did you know that I fell into the water?" Lucy's voice rang out, addressing nobody in particular. "I don't remember how I got out, but I did."

"It was Aunt Daisy who rescued you," Ellen said. "You should thank her properly."

Lucy scrambled down, knocking the dictionaries to the floor, ran toward Daisy, gave her a tight hug, and proclaimed, "I'm going to tell everybody in my class what you did."

A handful, thought Daisy, returning the hug. Enough spunk for two her age. Must keep Ellen hopping. Very, very sweet, all the same. Silly of me, but in a way now, I feel possessive about her.

"With every minute it becomes more incredible," Gene was saying. "What Daisy did! How can I ever express or thank . . . all of you . . . If I live to be a hundred . . . Excuse me." And with some embarrassment he wiped his eyes.

Awkwardly, Lewis patted his brother's arm. "That's all right. You already did, and we all know. We know."

Aaron, who sat across from the two men, was surprising himself with his own reflections. Funny, I never imagined that men like these would show tears. All that stiff-upper-lip business. Of course, I don't ever get this close. It's another world. Same city, but another world. And yet, here we sit with the same feelings—that little girl, that little mother today—we sit here feeding ourselves, all hungry, same stomachs, same bones, as I should know. The few times I ever saw the older one, I had no particular opinion one way or the other. He was a gentleman, that was all. Cool. Both brothers the same, I see. The only difference is, the first one's daughter didn't marry my son. It looks as if they're getting together. I hope so for Annette's sake. Their sakes too. This business in a family is wrong. Wrong.

"For the rest of my life," Gene was saying, "I'll have nightmares about what could have happened."

"Well, it didn't," Lewis said. "And as for nightmares, we've both had our share of them, I guess."

As his words carried, talk ceased. Annette, who had been talking to Brenda, pricked up her ears. Daisy, who had begun to say something cordial to Andrew—for although she had been so furious with him, he had been so kind to her today, as she had already told Cynthia—now stopped.

"Yes," Lewis repeated, "we've surely had plenty of them."

I admit to myself, he was thinking, that perhaps I was foolishly influenced after all. If it hadn't been for the Sprague family, the grandfather a judge, with all the prestige, I probably would have gone right in and demanded the truth. I would have raised hell.

"I seem to be having some second thoughts about things today," he said.

Gene nodded. "Yes, yes, I know what you mean. I guess circumstances alter cases, don't they? Cliché. But clichés are true."

And he wondered whether it was indeed possible that Jerry Victor really was a troublemaker with his own private agenda. Not that, if he had been, it would have altered the fact that Sprague had obviously been guilty; it would only in part have explained some of Lewis's reluctance to challenge Sprague. Perhaps, if Sprague had been my friend, I, too, would have hesitated. I have been quick to condemn. I have been closing my mind against Lewis, without even trying to understand, or forgive.

Annette watched her two sons. It must have been hard for Gene to be second all the time, always having to wait, being the younger, for the privileges of age, even to wait to go into the business. Of course, it couldn't have been otherwise, but still, that can put a chip of envy on a younger brother's shoulder. Then the older one sees the chip . . .

And suddenly words came out of her mouth, words she had certainly not intended to say.

"You've been too proud to talk things out, both of you. Too proud. Your father was like that too."

"The first time you ever said anything critical about Dad!" exclaimed Lewis.

"Well, what did you think? That he was perfect? Who is, pray tell me? Pride," she repeated, almost angrily.

" 'A man's pride shall bring him low,' " said Aaron, " 'but he that is of a lowly spirit shall attain to honor.' "

"Aaron!" Brenda wailed. "What on earth is wrong with you?"

"There's nothing wrong with him. That's from the Bible," Daisy said. "My father always quoted from the Bible."

"But the time and place!" Then, in spite of herself, Brenda had to laugh. "I'll tell you what, he's had too much wine."

" 'Wine is a mocker and strong drink is riotous,' " retorted Aaron with a wink.

At that the laughter was so loud that Jenny peeked through the kitchen door, smiled, and shook her head in amazement.

"I want to dance," said Lucy. "We always dance."

Ellen explained. "Mark and I like to dance sometimes. We put on a CD and roll back the rugs. Lucy has her own CD. She wants to be a ballerina."

"What's Lucy's music?" Annette asked.

" *'Gaîté parisienne.'* Have you got it?"

"Oh, yes, but this rug doesn't roll back."

"That's all right, I'll dance in the hall," said Lucy.

She was getting too much attention, Ellen knew, but today, why not? Today, she could have anything.

So the music started. Everyone stood up and watched Lucy perform. Filled with a sense of her own importance, but even more so with rhythm, she twirled her skirt and curved her arms above her head.

"Who'll dance with me?" she cried.

"I will," said Aaron in prompt response.

And, adorned with safety pins, with one hand

holding his trousers up and the other hand in Lucy's, he whirled with her down the length of the hall and back.

"What a good sport!" Daisy whispered to Annette in the midst of the general laughter. "I have to take my thoughts back. Both of them seemed so awkward and out of place this morning in the library, as if they resented being here."

"You never know about people till you know them," Annette responded.

She was thinking about Daisy. Who could say what quirk or insecurity had made Daisy put on what Annette called her "airs"? But so good, so incredibly brave . . . And she took Daisy's hand in a warm squeeze.

"Come, Mark and Ellen, join us," cried Aaron. You can see how nice he is to Ellen, Gene thought. And the way he brought Lucy back to life. Of course, he's a doctor and you expect it, but still, the sight of him breathing life into her . . . And Brenda, the way she pitched in, making all those beds, bringing coffee and blankets . . .

Lucy called, "Come on, Papa Gene, you dance too."

Belva Plain

So Papa Gene joined the whirl and gallop until, at last, Aaron brought it to a stop.

"I'm out of breath. Besides, I'm tripping over my trousers. Gene's trousers, I should say."

"It's clear where my husband gets his sense of humor," Ellen remarked when they had all sat down again.

Mark shook his head. "Mine's not half as good as Dad's. The funny thing is that he's quite serious while he's being funny. And when he's really serious, angry about something—watch out! Right, Mom?"

"Oh, my. Men," said Brenda.

"Men," echoed Ellen.

"When men are angry, they're like babies," Daisy said.

It's like old times in this house, Annette was thinking, with a little normal jibing and a lot of hilarity. But what if we hadn't come so near to tragedy? It would be shameful if it had to take a tragedy to bring about peace.

No, she resolved. Stubborn as I am, I would have found a way. I know I would.

When the dessert, a fluffy white meringue with

strawberries, had been sliced and passed around, Mark stood up with his wineglass in hand.

"I'm proposing a toast to you, Gran. Let's face it, this morning we were all pretty upset because of your little plan." He smiled. "And now instead we need to apologize, to thank you and wish you a hundred and twenty years."

"Thanks, but a hundred will do very well. Seriously, I really took a chance, didn't I? Last night I was so scared that I called my friend Marian to come to my aid. And now look. I look at you all . . . I'd better stop before I get teary."

Yes, she looks, but not very long at me, thought Cynthia, nor at Andrew. You destroyed everything that I felt for you, she told him silently.

She looked at him quickly and looked away. He was staring down at his plate. He doesn't even know what he did, she thought. And my parents, who love me, do not really know either. I saw them talking to him before. What a total about-face! How can they do that? They are hoping I will go back to him. Oh, I saw my mother leaning on him up the hill to the house. He brought hot towels for her and a blanket and coffee. Very nice, very kind, but what has that got to do with me? When I look at Mark and Ellen, I am so glad for them. They deserve each other. And Dad, with Uncle Gene—I'm so glad for them too. It was time and past time. But all that, too, has nothing to do with what has happened to me.

They were rising from the table, Annette proposing, "Let's have coffee by the fire, or what's left of it."

In the library the fire was barely high enough to cast a pink glow on a wall of books that were themselves a mosaic of soft colors. The coffee service was on a table, along with an enormous heap of chocolate macaroons.

"My goodness!" exclaimed Annette. "Where did these come from?"

"From your old favorite bakery on the East Side," said Gene.

"Oh, you went there too?" That was Brenda.

"Ours are from there." That was Daisy.

"We each wanted to be different," said Ellen.

And then there was more laughter over the macaroons. Annette felt the warmth of all the silliness. Feeling the peace in the room, she watched and listened.

Brenda was examining the portraits. Ellen was showing an album of old photos to Lucy. Daisy was browsing through the bookshelves, and the men, all except Andrew, were in one corner, talking.

"I'm saving," she heard Mark say, "to buy into an uptown gallery. If I ever get enough together, it will be my dream come true. And I'd still have time to work on my book. I've got a publisher somewhat interested."

Gene remarked that it all sounded very worthwhile.

"Well, it may come true and it may not. Either way, we're okay, Ellen and I."

"Can't you get a loan?" asked Aaron.

"It's very hard to get one without a good deal of collateral."

For a few moments the two fathers looked at each other. Then Gene said, "This sounds like something that should be talked over some more."

"Very definitely," Aaron agreed. "It's a pity when a person has a real commitment to something and has to wait forever."

Lewis, who had been listening, remarked that

that was quite true. He himself had lately been missing his own commitment. He had been wanting to get back to it with someone, though on a much smaller scale.

"Not impossible, I should think," said Gene with a meaningful smile.

"It's time for bed," Ellen called. "Lucy's falling asleep."

"I think we all are," said Aaron. "We've had a strenuous day, to say the least."

Annette was the last to turn out the lights and go upstairs. "Look at Mother," she heard Lewis remark to Gene as she closed her door. "Look at the happiness on her face."

Oh, yes, she was happy. . . . Except for Cynthia . . . All evening she had tried to catch her glance, to convey a message and plea. But plainly, Cynthia wanted to hear no message or plea.

Oh, what is the matter with me? I want perfection, Annette thought as she lay down to sleep. That's what's the matter with me. As if this evening has not been enough, I want more. I want it all. And I get so impatient.

* * *

Up and down the hall, around the corner into the wing, which Cynthia could see from her window, all the bedroom doors had been closed for the night. This would be the first time in what seemed like years that she would be sleeping under the same roof as Andrew was. It came also to her mind that the first time they had both slept under this particular roof was the night of the party that Gran had given for them when they returned from their wedding trip.

It would be far better now to forget all that. Yet there were hours in every human being's life that refused to be obliterated: times of unspeakable horror like today's, or else times like the one in the photograph, so beautifully framed, that Gran, for some reason known only to her, had placed on the chest of drawers in this room. There they were, Andrew looking unfamiliar in the traditional black morning coat and striped trousers; she in clouds of white silk with ushers and bridesmaids ranked on either side, all smiling, and he and she so happy that the happiness had bubbled up and wet their eyes. She stood now in the light of the bedside lamp, staring at the picture.

What innocence—summer, flowers, and a bottle of champagne in the room, kisses and joy forever after. Thank God that we never know what will happen to us tomorrow, to say nothing of any farther future. We had all the smiles and approval, we had everything, while Ellen and Mark had to sneak away to flee the storms.

She went to the window. The sleet had ceased, so that the pond was clearly visible, gleaming out of the dimness like a coin found on a dusty street. And the whole evil scene reenacted itself: Ellen's anguish, her mother stripping her skirt off, Andrew on the brink, hauling the rope, the abandoned baby crying on the grass . . . The whole scene.

Afterward there beside the fire and then later at dinner, I should have been at one with them in relief and thankfulness. In my heart, of course, I was, yet in my heart there was also something that kept me apart like a stranger watching a drama. You hear a tragic story and tears come to your eyes because you are human, a decent human being who feels a deep compassion, but still you are alone.

Pushing the curtain aside, she saw that clouds

were slowly breaking apart and receding. Tomorrow might even be sunny. They would leave here as early as possible. Then her parents should return to Washington as soon as possible. She was not angry at them; she was only, and undeniably, hurt. And she thought again that they need not have been so cordial to Andrew. I'm going back to work, she thought. That's all I need. Work.

It was early yet, too early to sleep, but she had brought two books and could read comfortably in bed. This house, although it had never been her actual home, had always had the feel of a second, or other, home. Gran had a talent for giving comfort. In this room with its wide bed that was probably a hundred years old, the reading lamp was perfect, the down quilt was light, and there was a tiny flowering plant in a pot on the windowsill.

Tired as Cynthia was, she took a quick shower, laid out her clothes for the morning, and put on a warm bedjacket over her chiffon nightgown. These articles, she reflected as she put them on, came from a life, or rather parts of a life, that had been spent with a husband and a career. Now both of these had been left behind.

She had not been reading for very long when somebody, no doubt Gran, who often liked a short evening chat, tapped on the door. Most likely, too, Gran would be seeking reassurance of her forgiveness for today's "little trick." Poor Gran, who believed she could right everyone's wrongs. Smiling at the thought, Cynthia got up and opened the door.

"May I come in?" Andrew whispered.

"What are you thinking of?" she replied in a furious whisper. "No, you may not come in."

"Please, Cynthia. I already am halfway in."

She had opened the door wide, and indeed, he was so far into the room that she was unable to close it. Now Andrew closed it firmly and stood leaning against it.

"What are you doing? Taunting me because I can't make an outcry?"

"Make one if you want to. You have the right. I am, after all, invading your room. Only, it might seem rather odd, since technically I am still your husband and have my right to be in your room."

"Macho man. Very funny. Go on. Say what you want and get out."

He was looking her up and down. "I remember that nightgown. My favorite color, sky-blue."

She wanted to slap from his face its unreadable expression, a mix of sorrow and plea.

"You're disgusting. Go on, take full male advantage of the fact that you're seven inches taller and weigh sixty pounds more than I do. Go on, it's typical."

"Ah, Cindy, haven't we had enough of this? It's time to get over it. Long past time."

"Is this what you've come to tell me? You're wasting your energy and mine. I'm in the middle of a good book."

"Please, listen to me. I was as shocked as you were when we met here today. I'd given up trying to communicate with you after a policeman stopped me for loitering at your—and our—front door. Well, to be accurate, I had almost given up. So when Gran invited me today, I thought that maybe she had some news for me, some good news."

"It's too late for good news."

"Why is it too late? I should think that after what we've been seeing here today, you'd realize that it's never too late."

"For you and me, it is," she repeated.

"Don't include me, Cindy. When I saw you holding Freddie today, I remembered—"

"I know too well what you remembered. And I have that, too, and more than that, to remember." She wanted to hurt him, and in a strange, perverse way of which she was entirely aware and was unable to explain, she wanted to feel the hurt herself.

Andrew sat down. For a few minutes he bowed, holding his head in his hands, not speaking. He looks white, he looks thinner, she thought. He looks beaten, sitting there like that. Yet she still wanted to hurt.

"You're bringing it all back," she said, breaking the silence. "It's indecent to do this to me. Haven't you done enough?"

"That silly woman—do you think she meant anything, for God's sake? I don't even remember her name, if I ever knew it. I wouldn't recognize her if I were to fall over her now."

"You've told me that a few times before, I think. Are you going to leave this room, or are you going to sit here all night? I'm freezing, and I want to go back to bed."

"I'm not leaving, Cindy. I'll sit here all night if I have to. Go back to bed if you're cold."

"Back to bed with you in the room? You must be out of your mind!"

"Go. I'm not going to touch you. I don't attack women. That's not my thing."

"Really? That's interesting."

In the bed again, Cynthia drew up the quilt and propped the book against her raised knees.

"How could you have?" she burst out.

"Cindy . . . I make no excuse. I guess in that crazy moment I just needed to feel alive again. I'd been dead for so long."

"*You* had? And I? What had *I* been?"

"Dead too. But I believe, I hope, that if you had done what I did, I would forgive you."

Yes, dead, she thought. We had not made love for more than half a year. When your heart is broken, what's left of you breaks too.

"I make no excuse," he resumed. "I say again that I wronged you terribly, and I'm sorry. Yes, I was a little bit crazy."

"Dead and crazy at the same time? Very unusual."

He got up and stood by the bed. White and

thin, she thought again, like me. This has wrecked us both.

"You saw what happened today, and what else could have happened," he said. "The world is a dangerous place. But we don't stop living because it is."

"A noble philosophy," she answered bitterly.

"What else can I say, then, except ask you to try again?"

"I can't." She was trembling. "I can't go back to what there was before. Now let me sleep. Will you go now?"

He shook his head.

"What are you going to do? Sit up all night?"

"No. I shall sleep on the floor."

"Damn you. I'm going to turn off the light."

For a long time she lay awake. The hurt in her chest grew with the suffocating weight of memories: the twins, the agony, the betrayal.

The clock on the stair landing chimed once. One o'clock. She had perhaps dozed for a little while; it was often impossible to distinguish between true dreams and waking dreams. There was no sound in the room, not even a rustle. He had probably crept away while she dozed. She reached to the lamp and turned it on.

There he lay, asleep on the floor at the foot of the bed. He had removed his jacket and, in his fastidious way, much like her own, had hung it over the back of a chair. The room was too cold to be lying there on the floor in his shirtsleeves. From the easy chair in the corner she took an afghan, most likely one of those that Gran's mother had knitted, and laid it over him.

He did not wake. She stood there looking at him. He lay perfectly straight, flat on his back, as people lie in their coffins. The wedding ring was gone from his left hand; it had been his idea to have a double-ring ceremony. He needed a shave. By the end of the day he always needed another shave.

It was odd to think that she was the only person in the whole world who knew everything about him, or as much as you can ever know about another human being. She knew that his eyes filled whenever there was a lost dog in a book or a movie. She knew that he carried a toothbrush in his attaché case, and that in private, at home, he often ate with his fingers.

An entirely illogical swell of pity moved in her throat.

I heard him get up, said Marian. *I heard him walk across the room and fall.* Then she said something like: *We wasted so much time.*

You have been too proud, Annette said.

And Aaron quoted, *"A man's pride shall bring him low."*

Shivering in the chill, she kept standing there.

Damn you. She was so angry. Damn you, she said without making a sound, while tears rolled down her cheeks.

In his sleep he must have become aware of her presence, for he opened his eyes, blinking into the lamplight. Startled then, he sat up.

"Is there anything wrong?"

"I covered you, that's all."

He was looking at her tears, while she looked at his hands. They were blistered and raw.

"Your hands," she said.

"Rope burns. It's nothing."

"Have they been like that all day? Why didn't you ask for something?"

"I don't know. It seemed unimportant with so much else happening."

"I have no Vaseline, but face cream should help for the time being."

He got up, sat on the bed, and stretched out his hands. Her tears were still brimming, while, with soft fingertips, she anointed them.

When she was finished, he gave her a long, steady look, and took her into his arms.

"Damn you," she said, and began to laugh.

"We'll begin again, Cindy. We can have everything again. Believe me. Everything. Do you understand?"

"Yes."

"Darling, turn out the light. We've waited so long."

A December sky, thought Annette, can be as deeply blue as any sky in May. So it was, in the morning as the house emptied out. In the front hall after breakfast they were gathering their coats and possessions.

"I was thinking," Gene whispered, "about your friend Marian. You may think this is foolish, but you know, in a certain way, she reminds me of Susan."

"Not foolish at all. A little tartness and a lot of sweetness. Yes, I see the resemblance."

"Perhaps I will give her a call sometime. Invite her to the theater or something."

Rather touched and a little amused by her son's apparent shyness, Annette replied quickly, "Of course. Why not?"

They were loading the cars. Lewis and Daisy were to drive back together, while Cynthia was to go with Andrew. You had only to look at those two to know that they had slept together. Nevertheless, Cynthia, wanting to make sure that she knew, had hugged her and whispered, "Thanks," in her ear.

Annette had winked. "Okay?"

"Yes, Gran, very okay."

And so they all departed. She stood watching them roll down the driveway and down the road until they were out of sight. Turning, then, to look back up at the house, she was reminded of Robert Frost's lines: *Home is where, when you have to go there, they have to take you in.* Well, none of my people *had* to come here; it's I who wanted to take them in. And she wondered whether it needed a tragedy to make people value the treasures of home and love. I hope not, she answered herself, but maybe, sometimes, it does.

Back in the library she paused before her husband's portrait.

"Well, Lewis," she said aloud, "we've had a few troubles since you left us. They're straightened out now, you'll be glad to know. Oh, I'm not naive enough to think, for instance, that Gene and Aaron will become close, dear friends; their ways and paths are too far apart for that. But at least they accept each other now, so when they meet it will seem natural, and the children will not suffer from the poison of anger. And our sons are together again, thank God. Thank Him for Ellen and Lucy, for Andrew and Cynthia. Thank Him for everything."

Outdoors, ice was dripping glitter from the trees, and the sun was brightening toward noon. The day was splendid.

"Come, Roscoe, let's take a walk," she said. "Come, boys. I'll get my coat. Let's go."